SHOOT FIRST,
ASK QUESTIONS LATER ...

Clint turned at the sound of the shot, instinctively knowing that Roosevelt was the target. As he turned he saw a man standing behind him, frozen for a moment, and then the man pulled his gun from inside his jacket.

Clint's hand went into his own jacket, grabbed for the gun in his shoulder holster, and pulled. The hammer caught on the inside fabric of the jacket, almost costing him his life.

The other man had obviously drawn his gun from a shoulder holster before, and he had allowed for the fabric of the jacket. He pointed his gun at Clint and fired. Clint dropped into a crouch, yanked his own gun free with a tear, and fired.

The other man's shot missed, going over his head.

Clint's shot did not miss . . .

THE GUNSMITH

SHOWDOWN AT LITTLE MISERY

J. R. ROBERTS

JOVE BOOKS, NEW YORK

SHOWDOWN AT LITTLE MISERY

A Jove Book / published by arrangement with
the author

PRINTING HISTORY
Jove edition / January 1998

The Putnam Berkley World Wide Web site address is
http://www.berkley.com

ISBN: 0-515-12210-6

A JOVE BOOK®
Jove Books are published by The Berkley Publishing Group, a member
of Penguin Putnam Inc.,
200 Madison Avenue, New York, New York 10016.
JOVE and the "J" design are trademarks
belonging to Jove Publications, Inc.

PRINTED IN THE UNITED STATES OF AMERICA

10 9 8 7 6 5 4 3 2 1

PART ONE
New York City
May

PROLOGUE

The man behind the big oak desk stared at Lamont, who had been standing nervously in front of the desk, waiting for his boss to acknowledge his presence.

His boss was an important man in New York banking, as well as other industries, and Lamont had been working for him for twelve years. Still, the aura of power that emanated from the man always made Lamont nervous.

"This is intolerable," the man growled.

"Yes, sir."

"We'll have to do something about it."

"Yes, sir."

"Shut up, Lamont."

"Yes, sir."

The man threw him a furious glare, and Lamont shut up immediately.

"Tomorrow the Brooklyn Bridge opens," the man said. "I want him to die there."

"Sir?"

"You heard me."

"At the ceremony?" Lamont asked incredulously.

"Yes," the man said, "at the ceremony. Get someone who can do it quietly."

Quietly, Lamont thought. That meant a knife.

"Sir—"

"What is it?"

"It's going to cost some money to get someone on short notice."

"Get it done, Lamont."

"Yes, sir."

"Now get out."

"Yes, sir."

"And stop saying 'yes sir' all the time. What are you, a goddamned yes-man?"

"Yes, sir."

"Oh, just get out."

"Yes—" Lamont started, then stopped and fled the office.

At last, the man behind the desk thought. He was annoyed that it had taken him this long to come to this decision, but it was finally done. He stood up, turned, and looked down at Wall Street from his window. After tomorrow, he wouldn't have Theodore Roosevelt to worry about any longer.

ONE

The Brooklyn Bridge was impressive, to say the least. The stone towers of the bridge stood 1,595 feet and six inches apart, effectively making it the longest suspension bridge in the world. At its center, at high tide, it stood 135 feet high above the water.

As anticipated, opening day—May 24, by coincidence also the birth date of Queen Victoria—was a gala affair, attended by newspapermen, politicians, Masons, local dignitaries, and celebrities. President Chester A. Arthur himself was on hand, and while the festivities were boycotted by a boat full of Irishmen for reasons of their own, this did little to dampen the Mardi Gras atmosphere on both sides of the bridge.

Clint Adams chose to observe the goings-on from the Manhattan side of the bridge. He'd been to Manhattan several times in the past, and to Brooklyn very few times. Although the bridge was called "The Brooklyn Bridge," he contented himself with the sights on the Manhattan side.

One of those sights was Jane Evergreen, the lady who was on his arm. She was a sight to rival the bridge itself, evidenced by the fact that many men tore their eyes from the stone structure to observe the more natural structure Clint wore on his arm.

Jane was tall, standing near five nine, and she was what most people would call a "full-bodied" woman. In truth, she was impressively built, but tall enough so that the thrust of hips and bosom served only to whet men's appetites and inflame their imaginations. Her flowing hair was flaming red and rested on her creamy white shoulders. The green gown she wore was cut as low as propriety would allow—and then a bit lower— to reveal soft, freckled breasts that swelled dangerously to overflowing.

Her face, lightly freckled, was full-lipped; her nose just slightly upturned. Her eyes were a dazzling green which dimmed the emeralds she wore around her throat.

In addition to being quite beautiful, Jane Evergreen was also quite wealthy. She and Clint were both staying at the famed Biltmore Hotel, and had met there several nights earlier. They had been sharing their nights—and much of their days—ever since.

Clint had been in Manhattan on several earlier occasions when the bridge was still under construction. When he read that the bridge was scheduled to open on May 24, he decided to come back to New York City and see it.

Now it was open, the ceremony having been presided over not only by the President of the United States, but by the mayor of New York and a long line of lesser politicians. The governor of New York sent along his regrets, and his lieutenant governor in his place.

"And now," Jane Evergreen said, squeezing Clint's arm tightly, "the parties begin."

"And how many are you invited to?" he asked, smiling at her.

"Oh, most of them," she said, touching her upper lip with the tip of her tongue. It was an affectation which might have been annoying on some other woman. On Jane it just served to wet her upper lip, making it glisten and appear even more delectable-looking . . . if that was possible. "And I suspect the ones I'm not invited to are not worth attending."

"I suspect you're right. Which one is first on the agenda?"

"The one at the Waldorf," she said, tightening her hold on his arm. "But we have to go back to the hotel first."

"What for?"

"This party is black tie."

"I don't have a black tie."

"I mean a tuxedo, silly," she said.

"I know what you mean," he said, "and I don't have one of those either."

"Yes, you do."

"I do?"

She nodded.

"I had one delivered to your room today," she said, "complete with top hat."

"A *top* hat?"

"Of course."

He frowned.

"I've never worn a top hat."

"You'll look stunning," she said. "Take my word for it."

"I'll try it all on," he said, "but that isn't to say I'll go out in public in it."

"You'll look wonderful."

"We'll see."

"I guarantee it."

"Is that a fact?"

She nodded, smiling.

"And if I don't?"

"If you don't agree that you look wonderful," she said, "you can have anything you want."

"Anything?"

"Anything."

"And if I do approve of the way I look?"

Her smile broadened and she said, "Then I get anything I want."

He started looking around frantically and said, "Where's a cab?"

Dignitaries were coming down from the dais as Clint and Jane tried to find a cab. Clint noticed a man moving furtively through the crowd, unlike everyone else, most of whom were simply bulling their way through.

"Jane," he said, "wait here."

"What is it?"

"Just stand still for five minutes."

"Clint—"

But he was gone, bulling his way through the crowd, moving sideways as they were moving forward, which made it that much more difficult.

Instinct told Clint that the man was up to no good.

There were plenty of police around, but no one seemed to be paying this particular man much attention. He was obviously heading for someone in particular, but Clint couldn't tell who. He only hoped he caught up to him in time to stop him before he . . . well, did whatever he was going to do.

For all Clint knew the man was simply a pickpocket, but as he got closer he saw the man's hand, and the knife that was clutched in it.

Clint started to shout, but there was too much noise for anyone to hear. The dignitaries were starting to split up and pile into cabs, and Clint could finally see who the man with the knife was after. He was a fit man in his forties, someone Clint knew had spoken earlier, but he couldn't remember the man's name.

He pushed hard, and suddenly—as if fate had decreed it—the crowd parted and Clint could see a clear path to the man with the knife. He sprinted just as the blade man reached his quarry and drew back his arm for a fatal strike. Clint reached out and managed to grasp the man's wrist just before he could make his final thrust.

"Hold it!" Clint shouted.

The man turned. He was small and wiry, which was probably why he had been chosen for the job.

His intended victim had gotten into a cab and was no longer within reach.

"Son of a bitch!" the small man yelled, and kicked Clint in the shin.

"Ow!" Clint shouted, and the man slipped from his grasp and disappeared into the crowd.

Clint stood there for a moment, looking around. No one had seen a thing, not any of the onlookers or any of the uniformed police, and both of the parties involved were gone. There was nothing to do but go back to Jane.

"Where did you go?" she asked when he returned.

"I thought I saw someone I knew."

"Why are you limping?"

"I bumped my leg."

"Poor baby," she said. "I know how to make you feel better."

He smiled and said, "Let's find that cab," and the incident was forgotten.

TWO

Clint and Jane separated in the lobby of the Biltmore to go to their respective rooms and change for the evening of party hopping. Jane said she always took a room here when there were parties to go to.

As promised, when Clint entered his room, he saw the tuxedo laid out on his bed. It had taken him only a day to get used to having Jane spend money on him. Since she had so much of it, he decided—after some soul-searching—that if it made her happy, he wasn't going to argue with her.

Also in the room, sitting on the chest of drawers next to the bed, was the top hat he was to wear. Shaking his head, he walked over to it and picked it up. He'd seen men in top hats before, in England, and in San Francisco. In fact, he'd once seen his own good friend, Bat Masterson, wear one. Bat, however, had the bearing to pull off such a feat. Clint didn't know if he had, but he was willing to find out.

Unhurriedly, he removed his clothes and donned the tuxedo. Checking himself in the mirror, he found that he approved of the way he looked. But the ultimate test was still to come—the top hat.

It was flattened out now, obviously brand-new and never worn before. He slapped it against his palm and the top popped out. He'd seen Bat do the same thing—and Luke Short, too, come to think of it—and was surprised that he'd been able to accomplish it on the first try.

Gingerly, he set the hat atop his head, then stood in front of the mirror and took a good look.

He looked damned good, even if he admitted it himself. He supposed there were worse things than losing a bet to Jane Evergreen—especially when you considered how this particular bet was structured.

Satisfied with the tuxedo and top hat look, Clint picked up his little Colt New Line hide-out gun and the shoulder rig he had bought for it. He'd seen Bat and Luke and some others—Doc Holliday was another—wear these shoulder holsters, but he had never tried one himself. He'd been wearing one for the past three days, however, beneath his regular jacket, and was just starting to become comfortable with it. The New Line was light and compact and fit perfectly into the holster, and the gun didn't show beneath his regular jacket.

He removed his tuxedo jacket, slipped into the shoulder rig, hitched it about until he was comfortable, then slipped the jacket back on. Another look in the mirror told him that the gun didn't show at all. Jane had probably bought the jacket from some outrageously expen-

sive tailor shop, because the fit—even with the gun—
was perfect.

Taking one last look at himself in the mirror, he nodded with satisfaction and left the room to go down to
the hotel bar to await Jane's arrival.

In the barroom he leaned against the expensive ma-
hogany bar—polished to a shine—and ordered a beer.

"Mr. Adams!"

He turned at the sound of his name and saw a man
approaching him. It was a man he'd met recently, over
the past few days he'd spent with Jane, and he groped
for the name as the speaker approached.

"How are you, sir?" the man asked, extending his
hand.

"Fine . . . Mr. Sprague," Clint said, finding the name
at the last moment, "just fine. Can I buy you a drink?"

"Well, yes, I don't mind if I do have one."

The man was in his early forties, and Clint remembered that he was some kind of politician—an assemblyman. Jane had introduced them one night when they
had run into him at a place called Clark's Tavern.

When the bartender came with Clint's beer, Sprague
ordered one, as well.

"Were you at the opening, sir?" Sprague asked.

"I was there," Clint said.

"It's a magnificent structure, isn't it? The Brooklyn
Bridge?"

"Breathtaking."

"Well," Sprague said, laughing, "let's not go that
far. The only thing I've seen in the past few days that
is breathtaking is the young lady you had on your arm
the other night."

"Jane is beautiful," Clint said.

"Yes, sir, indeed she is," Sprague said. "In fact, I would like to propose a toast to Miss Evergreen's beauty, if I may."

The two men drank the toast, and then Sprague thanked Clint for the drink and drifted away.

"Still a lot of handshaking to do," the man said. "A politician's work is never done."

Clint agreed to let the man go and shake the hands that would do him the most good. He found Sprague—and most politicians—tedious after a very short time.

Clint knew when Jane entered the bar without even seeing her. It grew very still as all conversation ceased. He turned and saw her at the entrance, a vision in a low-cut blue gown that showed even more of her breasts than the previous green number had. All eyes were on her as she walked toward Clint, smiling broadly, her hips adopting a very exaggerated and deliberate sway. Her breasts bounced, as well, and Clint knew that this could only have been achieved by the total disregard of undergarments on her part.

By the time she reached him he was aroused, as was every other man in the room.

"Don't you look dapper," she said, putting her hand on his arm and kissing his cheek.

"Yes, I do."

"You agree?"

"I do."

"Then I win the bet?"

"You win," he said. "I look great."

"Yes, you do," she said. "Come then. We have

places to go, and people to see, before we come back here and I . . . collect on my bet.''

"I can't wait.''

She took his arm and they walked out of the bar together, Clint Adams the envy of every man there.

THREE

They stopped at a couple of small parties along the way, but the main party was the one at the Waldorf. That, Jane said, was the party where everyone would be seen, the one that would be in the society pages the next day. Politicians, artists, actors and actresses, the idle rich . . .

". . . and you and me," she finished, as they stepped out of the carriage in front of the hotel.

"How long do we have to stay here?" he asked.

"As long as it takes me to show you off," she said, "in your tuxedo and top hat."

"I'm starting to feel like I'm on display," Clint said.

"You are," she said, squeezing his arm. "Just consider this part of my collecting on my bet."

They went inside and made their way to the Grand Ballroom, where musicians were playing and people were either milling about or dancing. There was no formal bar, but waiters were circulating carrying trays of complimentary champagne.

Clint grabbed two glasses from a passing waiter and handed Jane one of them.

"Lawyers," she said, looking around, "doctors, ex-mayors, businessmen . . . they're all here."

"It's an impressive turnout, all right," Clint agreed. "What do we do now?"

"Circulate, darling," Jane said.

"Together, or separately?"

"Both. Let's split up while I make contact with some of the, uh, more important women who are present. Maybe you can find a man with a cigar."

One of the things Clint liked about Jane was her irreverence toward established conventions. She thought that men with their men-only clubs and cliques were funny, and that the huge cigars that many of the men in public life affected were even funnier.

She branched off and went to talk to a group of women who had gathered off to one side, certainly the wife of a politician or two and some society matrons, as well. Clint sipped his champagne and walked around, then stopped when he saw a man coming toward him. He'd seen Assemblyman Sprague once already tonight, and didn't know what else he'd have to say to the man, but there was no avoiding him.

"Ah, Mr. Adams," Sprague said, "somehow I knew you'd be here."

"Mr. Sprague—"

"And where is the lovely Miss Evergreen?"

"She's around."

"I wonder if you would mind doing me a favor, sir."

"And what would that be, Mr. Sprague?"

"There's a gentleman here who would very much like to meet you," Sprague said. "I wonder if you'd allow me to make the introductions."

"Why not?" Clint said. "I understand that's why we're all here, to see and be seen with people."

"Excellent. If you would come with me?"

As they walked along Clint asked, "Who is this man, anyway?"

"One of my younger colleagues—and, in fact, our youngest assemblyman. His name is Theodore Roosevelt."

Clint frowned. It seemed to him he knew the name, either having heard it or read it in a newspaper. He commented on this.

"Oh, yes, I'm sure you've both heard and read it," Sprague said. "He has a very big future ahead of him, does our young Mr. Roosevelt."

They continued to make their way across the massive ballroom, stopped along the way by men who wanted to shake the assemblyman's hand or whisper in his ear. In no case did Sprague bother making any sort of introduction.

Finally they reached a group of men, at the core of which stood a strapping young man—not tall, but the kind of man who projected an energy that affected the people around him. It was easy to see that he was the center of attention, and thriving on it.

"Excuse me," Sprague said, making his way through the group with Clint in tow, "excuse me—Theodore . . . Teddy . . . Theodore Roosevelt—" They had finally reached him and gotten his attention. "—I'd like you to meet Clint Adams. Mr. Adams, this is Theodore Roosevelt.''

Before Clint could say anything, Roosevelt grabbed his hand and started pumping it, talking at the same time.

"This is a real honor, sir, a genuine pleasure to meet you. I've heard so much about you—gentlemen, gentlemen, this man is a genuine legend of the old West, right up there with Wild Bill Hickok—could you give us some time? Thank you, thank you, we'll talk again. . . .''

Clint was surprised at his reception, and surprised at how quickly Roosevelt got the men to disperse, leaving them virtually alone in the huge ballroom. He also found Roosevelt to be very familiar to him, although he couldn't place where he might have seen him.

"I hope I didn't embarrass you," Roosevelt said.

"Embarrass is not the word I would use, Mr. Roosevelt," Clint said.

"I understand," Roosevelt said. "You would like to keep a low profile."

"Exactly."

"I apologize, then," Roosevelt said. "It's just that I'm very excited to meet you. I wonder . . . would you prefer a real drink to that bubbly water?"

Clint looked at the champagne glass in his hand, which was still mostly full.

"As a matter of fact, I would."

"So would I."

Roosevelt snagged a passing waiter, took Clint's glass and placed it with his own on the tray, and waved the man away.

"Come with me," Roosevelt said. "I know just the place."

FOUR

Clint was surprised when Roosevelt led him out of the hotel via a back door, and down a dark, barely lit street until they reached a saloon easily missed if you didn't know it was there—and Roosevelt obviously did.

"Beer?" he asked Clint as they entered.

"That's fine."

"Two beers, Charlie," Roosevelt called out to the saloon keeper, "in the back."

He led Clint through a small, well-furnished, dimly lit front room where men were sitting, drinking, and conversing quietly. Several of them nodded to the young politician, who returned the nods wordlessly.

As they entered the back room Roosevelt removed his jacket. Clint saw that the room was dominated by a green felt billiard table, set right in the center of the room.

"Do you play?" Roosevelt asked.

"Some."

In truth, Clint had touched a pool stick—or cue—only rarely, but he knew the rudiments of the game. The Earps had played fairly frequently while in Tombstone, and he had watched. It seemed to him that the same attributes that made a man good with a gun—a sharp eye and a steady hand—could be put to good use when playing pool.

There were pool sticks on a rack on the wall, and Roosevelt walked to it and plucked two.

"Here you are," he said. "That's a fine stick."

Clint could see that the stick was straight, so he just said, "Thanks."

The bartender entered the room with two frosty mugs of beer as Roosevelt was firing up a cigar. Clint took one and Roosevelt accepted the other with a sigh of relief.

"To your health," he said to Clint and took a healthy swig.

Clint did the same.

"Cigar?" Roosevelt asked.

"No, thanks."

"Too many people at that party, wouldn't you say?"

"There were a lot."

Roosevelt set his beer down on the side of the table and then racked all fifteen balls.

"Make it interesting?" he asked.

"What did you have in mind?"

"A dollar a ball?"

"Done."

"First to two hundred wins," Roosevelt said. "We should be able to do that before we're missed."

Clint wasn't sure that was true, but there was something about this young man—something magnetic—that held you in his presence. He wondered if Jane would understand that when he explained it to her in a couple of hours.

"All right."

"Let's lag for break."

Each man took a ball, hit it to the cushion at the other end. Each ball bounced off and came back, bounced off their cushion, and Roosevelt's stopped closest to the cushion.

"Bully," he said, "I break. No need to call our pockets, since it's a friendly game."

Clint decided if Roosevelt thought that a dollar a ball was a friendly game, he wouldn't have wanted to play the man in earnest.

Clint stepped back and watched as Roosevelt sent all fifteen balls scattering, two of which—the one and the twelve—went into pockets. The man proceeded to shoot, rerack, and shoot again before he missed after sinking twenty-four balls.

"Your shot," he said, stepping back.

Clint moved to the table and studied the remaining six balls. Apparently, Roosevelt did not talk while he was shooting, but it did not bother him to talk while someone else was.

"Have you any interest in politics, Mr. Adams?" he asked as Clint continued to study the table.

"Not really, Mr. Roosevelt."

"Please," Roosevelt said magnanimously, "my friends call me Teddy."

"And mine call me Clint."

Clint leaned over and calmly sank a ball, banking it off a cushion first.

"Nice shot," Roosevelt said. "You have played before."

"Not very much," Clint said, sinking a ball dead-on, "but I've watched some friends play."

"Oh? And who might that have been?"

"The Earps," Clint said. "Morgan and Virgil more than Wyatt."

"In Tombstone?"

"That's right."

Clint sank a third ball and then turned his head to look at Roosevelt. The man's eyes were shining behind rimless eyeglasses, the smoke from his cigar floating around his head, and suddenly—while shooting and shooting well—Clint found himself regaling Roosevelt with tales of the old West—some true, and some exaggerated.

The young politician was so enamored that he barely noticed that Clint continued to shoot balls into the pockets until, finally, Clint stood up and stopped talking and shooting.

Roosevelt looked at the table, saw that there were still balls there, and asked, "Is something wrong?"

"That's two hundred," Clint said to his new friend. "You owe me one hundred and seventy-six dollars, Teddy."

Roosevelt frowned at the table for a few moments, then looked at Clint and asked, "You didn't miss a shot?"

"I was lucky," Clint said.

Roosevelt stuck his hand into his pocket, came out with some money, and said, "Bully."

FIVE

"It was worth every penny," Roosevelt said as he and Clint reentered the Waldorf's Grand Ballroom. "Sir, the stories you tell, they're . . . exciting. More exciting than anything I could experience here in New York, I tell you. The world of politics—"

"Has its own pitfalls, I imagine," Clint said.

The two men came to a stop and Roosevelt looked at Clint.

"Yes, it does," he said, "it certainly does." He stuck his hand out and Clint took it. "Clint, since I played hooky for two hours I'm afraid I have to mingle. It was a pleasure to be in your company."

"I enjoyed it, Teddy."

"And perhaps you'll give me a chance to get even sometime, eh?" Roosevelt asked. "If not at pool then perhaps . . . poker?"

"It would be my pleasure."

"Splendid." Roosevelt released Clint's hand and straightened his jacket. "Once more into the breach . . ." he said, and moved into the crowd.

Clint snagged a glass of champagne from a passing waiter and then saw Jane approaching him. He steeled himself for a scolding.

"Can I have a sip?" she asked.

"Sure."

She took his glass, drank half the champagne, and gave it back.

"Those women could talk the spots off a tablecloth," she said, shaking her head. "I'm sorry I kept you waiting so long."

Clint smiled to himself. Obviously, she had never noticed that he was gone.

"It was only a couple of hours."

"Oh, was it?" she asked. "You poor dear. Were you terribly bored?"

"I . . . managed to amuse myself," he said, aware of Theodore Roosevelt's one hundred and seventy-six dollars lining his pocket.

"Well, let's just walk around together for a little while," she said, hooking her arm in his, "and then we can go back to the hotel so I can collect on my wager."

"That sounds good to me," Clint said.

"And maybe we can manage to find a waiter," she added as they started walking, "so I can have a glass of champagne of my own."

SIX

They mingled only for another half hour and then returned to the Biltmore, where they retired to Jane's room, not his.

"My bet," she said as they went up the stairs, "my room."

"No argument."

When they got to her room she didn't bother to turn the lamp up. She turned and came into his arms, her sweet mouth seeking his, her body pressed tightly to his.

"Help me with my gown," she said against his mouth. He didn't need to be told twice. In no time the gown was at her feet, and he could see—and feel—that he had been correct when he assumed she was wearing no undergarments.

She pressed her naked body to him again, and he ran his hands down over her back to her buttocks, which were firm and rounded. Her tongue sought his as he squeezed her ass, kneading it so that she moaned into his mouth.

She pulled away from him then and held his hands.

"Come," she said, pulling him toward the bed, "it's time to get you out of your tuxedo now."

He couldn't wait. He'd worn one before, but it had been a while, and he'd forgotten how uncomfortable they could be when you wore one for hours.

He stood still as she undid his tie, and then his shirt, sliding it off of him and dropping it to the floor. She ran her hands over his chest, kissed his nipples, then got on her knees and undid the trousers, sliding them down his legs. She pushed him down on the bed so she could remove his boots, then finished with the trousers. All that was left was his underwear, and he lifted his hips so she could get to that. His penis was hard and ready, and she pounced on it, holding it in her hands, cooing to it, finally licking it until it was good and wet, and then taking it into her mouth.

He watched as her head bobbed up and down as she sucked him, loudly and wetly, moaning her appreciation. It was obvious that she could feel how ready he was and she allowed him to slip from her mouth with one last lick.

"Lie back on the bed."

He did as he was told because, after all, it was her winning wager she was collecting on.

She crawled onto the bed with him, pressing herself to him, stroking his penis and then straddling his hips. His eyes had become accustomed to the darkness, and he reached for her breasts, palming them, squeezing them and flicking the nipples with his thumbs.

Breathing quickly, she reached between them, took hold of him, and guided him up into her. They both gasped, she as he filled her up and he as he felt her heat envelop him. She began to move on him then, riding him up and down with her hands flat against his chest. The room filled with the sound of their quickened breathing, and then they were gasping as they moved together. Finally she cried out as her passion overtook her, and then moments later he almost roared as he ejaculated into her. It felt as if she were milking him, looking for more and more until he had no more to give, and then she collapsed on him, licking the sweat from his neck and saying into his ear, "That was wonderful . . . for a start."

She woke him later by sliding down between his legs and licking him until he opened his eyes. Then she smiled and lay down next to him, on her back.

"Your turn."

He knew what she wanted and it was his pleasure to give it to her. He started at her neck, kissing her, working his way down to her chest, kissing her breasts, skirting the nipples for now, kissing her shoulders, her right armpit, her right arm, then her hand. He continued down the right side of her body, along the hip, her thigh and her leg until he reached her foot. He positioned himself at the bottom of the bed and lifted her leg.

"Oh, God," she said, because she knew what was coming—and then he took her big toe into his mouth. She gasped and grabbed the sheet on either side of her as he sucked the digit. He'd never found a woman before who enjoyed having her toes sucked as much as Jane Evergreen did.

He moved from the big toe to the next one, and then the next one, to the small toe and then back again, and then he ran his tongue over her foot, which made her toes curl.

"Ooh yeah," she said breathlessly, "now the other one . . ."

He repeated the performance with the other foot, sucking her big toe wetly, only this time as he did it he slid one hand up her thigh until he could touch her wetness. He found her clit and teased it while he continued to suck her toe, and this pushed her right over the edge. She gasped and bit her lip to keep from screaming, but her fists released the sheet and she began to punch the bed.

Clint released her foot, straddled her, and entered her roughly before she could recover. She wrapped her legs around his waist then and held him tightly as he began to move in and out of her. He slid his hands beneath her so he could cup her buttocks, and as he drove into her he'd pull her to him so that he was plunging as deeply as possible into her.

"Ooh, Clint, yes, oh, God . . ." she moaned, holding him tighter still, wrapping her arms around him, raking his back with her nails until finally he exploded inside of her.

In the morning Clint woke Jane the way she had awakened him during the night, only when she opened her eyes he continued to lick her. She moaned and reached down to hold his head in place, afraid that he'd stop. There was no danger of that, though. He was enjoying himself too much to stop. Enjoying the way she tasted, and smelled, and the way she reacted to the ministrations of his tongue. Finally she tensed and then seemed to explode in a flurry of activity that made him have to fight to keep his mouth in contact with her. Finally she pushed him away, whispering, "Enough, enough . . . you're going to kill me."

He remained where he was and touched her with his hand. She jumped, because she was so sensitive now it almost hurt to be touched.

"Is the wager paid?" he asked.

"You bastard—" she started, but he just brushed her clit with his forefinger, and she gasped and closed her thighs over his hand, trying to get away from him.

"Is it paid?" he asked again.

"Yes, yes, yes, it's paid," she cried out. "You're an awful, awful man, Clint Adams . . . stop touching me!"

Finally, he withdrew, and she rolled over and curled herself into a ball, in self-defense.

"Awful . . ." she said.

SEVEN

Her opinion of him as "awful" lasted only a few more minutes before she rolled onto her back and accepted his kisses.

"I don't know how you do that," she said. "No man has ever given me so much pleasure that I'd push him away. If anyone had ever told me it could happen, I would have called them a liar."

"I'm a special man," he said.

"Oh, I know that well, Mr. Adams."

"Do you want breakfast?" he asked.

"God, no," she said. "I'd never be able to walk. You're hungry, aren't you?"

"Starving."

"Then you go," she said. "Have breakfast and go back to your room. You have to give me time to recover."

He kissed her and said, "I'll see you later this afternoon."

"Late in the afternoon," she said, rolling over and pulling the sheet up to her neck. "I need to get my beauty sleep."

He got to his feet and pulled on his wrinkled tuxedo. By the time he was ready to leave the room, she was breathing evenly, fast asleep. He decided he couldn't eat breakfast in this suit, so he went back to his room to change before going down to the hotel dining room.

When he reached the dining room, breakfast was in full swing. He was able, however, to get a table for one with no problem. He was a big tipper and the waiter, Walter, who had become his regular while he was there, found him a table with no problem.

"Will the lady be joining you this morning?" Walter asked. He was a young man in his twenties and obviously approved of Clint's choice of female companion. He all but tripped over his tongue whenever he served her.

"No, I'm afraid not, Walter," Clint said, "sorry to disappoint you."

"The usual for you?" Walter said, hiding his disappointment well.

"Sure, why not?"

Clint had taken to eating steak and eggs every morning while he was in New York.

"I'll bring your coffee right out."

"See if you can find me a newspaper, Walter," Clint said. "I'll need one since I'll be eating alone this morning."

"Yes, sir. Comin' up."

Walter reappeared moments later with a pot of coffee and a copy of *The New York Times*. The front page was filled with stories about and photographs of the Brooklyn Bridge. Clint read them while drinking two cups of coffee, and then when breakfast came he found himself on the society page—literally. He was mentioned twice, as having Jane Evergreen on his arm—or vice versa—and then again for being seen with Assemblyman Theodore Roosevelt. The paper made a point of mentioning that Roosevelt was the youngest assemblyman in New York history. It also mentioned that Clint Adams had a reputation in the old West as a "gunman, to rival that of Wild Bill Hickok."

Clint folded the newspaper and put it down. There was no point in getting upset about it. He knew that no matter how far north, south, east, or west he went in this country, his reputation was not something he could get away from.

He ate the remainder of his breakfast without reading the rest of the newspaper, and did not allow what he had read to ruin his meal.

Clint was working on his second pot of coffee when three men entered the dining room, looked around, spotted him and walked to his table.

"Are you Clint Adams?" one of the men asked.

"Who wants to know?"

The spokesman was in his forties and sported an anvil jaw. He reached into his jacket pocket and pulled out a badge.

"The name's Egan, Sergeant Egan, New York Police. Are you Adams?"

"I am. What can I do for you?"

"Mind if I sit?"

"Go ahead."

Egan sat across from Clint.

"What about your friends?"

"They'll stand."

"What can I do for you, Sergeant?"

"It's come to my attention that you and Teddy Roosevelt are friends."

"Have you been reading the papers?"

Egan's eyes went to the folded newspaper on the table.

"I've seen it."

"What the paper doesn't tell you is that I just met Roosevelt yesterday. That doesn't exactly qualify us as friends, does it?"

"I don't know," Egan said. "You tell me."

"What's your interest, Sergeant?" Clint asked. "Is it against the law to be Teddy Roosevelt's friend?"

Egan hesitated, then said, "Maybe to some people."

Clint had an odd feeling at that point. He felt that the two men who were standing were not Egan's subordinates. He also had a hunch they were not policemen, as Egan was.

"I understand you have a reputation with a gun," Egan said.

"You have been reading the papers."

"Does that mean you . . . hire your gun out?"

Clint leaned forward in his chair. He felt the two standing men lean slightly forward, as well. Egan seemed to hold his ground.

"No," Clint said, "that's not what it means."

"Are you a lawman, then?"

"No," Clint said. "I have been, but not for a long time."

"Would you hire your gun out . . . for the right price?"

Clint was about to reply angrily but thought better of it. Was the man questioning him as a lawman, or trying to hire him?

He sat back.

"I guess that would depend on what I was being hired to do," Clint said, "and for how much."

Egan nodded, then looked up at the other two men, one of whom also nodded.

"I guess I got what I wanted," Egan said, standing up.

"And what was that?"

"Somebody else might want to talk to you, Adams."

"I'll be around."

Egan looked at the other two men and said, "Let's go."

Clint watched them as they walked out, wondering if he'd just given them the impression that he could be hired out . . . to kill someone.

EIGHT

It didn't take Clint long to put it all together. The day after he'd been seen with Teddy Roosevelt he'd been approached about the possibility of hiring out his gun. Roosevelt being the youngest assemblyman in the history of the state, he was bound to have some enemies. When Egan left he'd said that someone else would want to talk to Clint. It seemed clear that someone was going to approach him about killing Theodore Roosevelt.

He could have answered Egan's questions differently, and the man probably would have gone away and not bothered him again. Instead, he'd allowed the policeman to think he might be available. His next step was to wait for the offer, and find out who it was coming from.

But perhaps not.

Maybe there were a couple of other things he could do first.

He could check on Egan, make sure the man truly was a New York City policeman.

Second, he could talk to Roosevelt and let him know what was going on. In fact, that might kill two birds with one stone. Roosevelt would certainly have the influence to check on Egan's credentials. Also, if Egan was a crooked policeman, Roosevelt would probably know how high the corruption in the police department went.

So, his next step, logically, seemed to be talking to Theodore Roosevelt. All he had to do was find out where the man lived.

He thought briefly about going upstairs and waking Jane up. She knew where everyone who was anyone in New York lived. He had second thoughts, however, when he saw the waiter, Walter, coming toward his table. Waiters knew almost as much as bartenders.

"Can I do anything else for you, Mr. Adams?" Walter asked.

"Yes, Walter," Clint said. "Did you see the three men who were just here?"

"Yes, sir, I did."

"Do you know them?"

Walter hesitated, and Clint dug into his pocket to pay for the information.

"Oh, no, Mr. Adams," the waiter said, "I'm not holdin' out for money."

"Then what?"

"Well . . . those men who were just here are dangerous."

"All of them?"

"Yes, sir."

"One of them said he was a policeman. Is he?"

"Oh, yes, sir," Walter said. "That was Sergeant Egan."

"Sergeant Egan did not strike me as the most honest of policemen, Walter."

"You could tell that by the company he keeps, sir."

"Those two men?"

"Yes, sir."

"Who do they work for?"

"Sir, if you don't mind . . ." Walter said, letting it trail off.

"All right, Walter," Clint said, "I won't try to force it out of you."

"Thank you, sir."

"Maybe you can help me with something else."

"If I can, sir."

"Do you know where Theodore Roosevelt lives?"

"Oh, sure," Walter said, "that's an easy one to answer. He lives at Tranquility."

"Tranquility? Is that a place, Walter?"

"It's his family's summer home," Walter said, "in Long Island. Mr. Roosevelt has lived there since he came back from gettin' married."

"Long Island."

"Yes, sir. Oyster Bay."

"Oyster Bay."

"Yes, sir."

"Doesn't he have a place in the city?"

"Yes, sir," Walter said, "they have a residence on Fifty-Seventh Street."

"That's what I want, then," Clint said. "Can you tell me exactly where it is?"

"I can give you an address, and I can direct you right to the door."

"That's what I want, Walter," Clint said. "I knew I came to the right man."

Walter gave him precise directions and described the house.

"It's number six, West Fifty-Seventh Street. It's a mansion designed by architect Russell Sturgis for Theodore Roosevelt, Senior."

"I didn't know there was a Senior."

"Oh, yes," Walter said, "and he is a very rich man. The Oyster Bay house is just one of the family homes, which he has turned over to his son and his wife, Alice."

"So she stays out there?"

"Yes," Walter said, "and when Teddy—everybody calls him that—is in town he stays at the Fifty-Seventh Street mansion. That's where you'll find him."

"Thanks, Walter."

Again, Clint started to go into his pocket.

"I don't take money for information," Walter said, but then he added—before Clint could remove his hand—"however, I do take tips for services."

"Fine service it was, too," Clint said, leaving a generous tip on the table.

NINE

Clint didn't know exactly who Russell Sturgis was, but he had done a fine job on the Roosevelt home on West Fifty-Seventh Street. For instance, he had no idea that while the house was in the normal "town house" style, the inside was quite richly furnished. The high ceilings were lined with real oak beams, and there was a large museum and a gymnasium inside.

Theodore Senior was only forty-two years old, in the prime of his life. He was the founder of the Metropolitan and Natural History museums and the patron of many New York charities.

Clint had no idea how young Theodore Senior was until the man answered the front door himself and introduced himself. He looked like Teddy would probably look in fifteen or twenty years, heavier, blockier, but extremely healthy-looking. At this point Clint had no knowledge of Teddy's sickly childhood.

"Come in, Mr. Adams, come in," the man said graciously. "Teddy has told me quite a bit about your meeting."

"Really?" Clint asked as Theodore Senior—he didn't know if he could even think of the man as "Teddy" Senior—closed the door behind him. "I wouldn't think there was that much to tell."

"Running two hundred balls in a row is quite impressive," the man said.

"Well . . ."

Now Clint knew why Teddy Roosevelt had seemed familiar to him. It was because he looked so much like his father, and it had been Theodore Roosevelt, Senior, whose life Clint had saved after the Brooklyn Bridge ceremony.

"Are you here to see Teddy?" Roosevelt asked, snapping Clint from his reverie.

"Er, as a matter of fact, I am," Clint said, wondering if he should tell the man what had happened at the ceremony. Would it do any good at this point?

"He's in the study. I believe he's working on a new bill or something. Come this way."

Clint followed the man down a hall to the study, where Teddy Roosevelt, Jr., sat in shirtsleeves behind a huge oak desk.

"Teddy, you have a visitor," Theodore Senior said. He looked at Clint and said, "I'll give you two some privacy. It was nice meeting you, Mr. Adams."

"And you, sir."

The older man—in truth, he was younger than Clint—

exited and closed the double doors behind him. They were also made of oak.

"Ah, Clint, my friend," Teddy said, bounding from behind the desk and pumping Clint's hand. "How nice of you to come. I'm, uh, somewhat busy at the moment, but I can give you a few minutes . . . is this visit business or pleasure?"

"Not pleasure," Clint said. "I wouldn't describe it that way. As to business . . . it concerns your safety, Teddy."

Roosevelt frowned.

"My safety. Well, that does sound like it deserves more than just a few minutes, doesn't it? Have a seat. Would you like a drink?"

"I don't think so. Thanks."

Teddy went back around the desk and said, "Let's get to it, then. What's this about my safety?"

"Well, I believe someone is going to try to hire me to kill you."

Teddy looked surprised but not shocked.

"And I assume you will not accept the job?"

"Of course not," Clint said, "but I made it seem as if I might."

"I don't understand," Teddy said. "You said someone was *going* to try to hire you. Has someone approached you already?"

"Yes."

"Who?"

"A man named Egan," Clint said. "He claimed to be a police officer, and he had the badge to back up his claim."

Teddy was nodding even before Clint finished.

"I know of Sergeant Egan, Clint."

"I understand he's somewhat . . . corrupt?"

"That's putting it mildly. Egan is possibly the most corrupt policeman on a force of corrupt policemen."

"Why is he a policeman, then?"

"Contacts," Teddy said, "in high places, both in the police department and in the criminal world."

"I see."

"Tell me about your meeting."

Briefly Clint described the meeting in the hotel dining room.

"I hope talking with Egan didn't ruin your breakfast," Teddy said when he was finished. "It was quick thinking of you to be vague."

"Do you have any idea who he was talking about when he said someone else would be wanting to talk with me?" Clint asked.

Teddy laughed shortly and said, "Could be a lot of people. I ruffle people's feathers, my friend."

"You should have security around you."

"I carry a gun," Teddy said. "In a shoulder holster, like the one you're wearing now."

Clint shrugged his shoulders and said, "I didn't think it showed."

"It doesn't," Teddy said, "but you're not yet comfortable with it. Besides, I saw it last night while we were shooting pool."

"You should still have a bodyguard."

"Fine," Roosevelt said, "I pick you."

TEN

"I can't be your bodyguard, Teddy."

"Why not?"

"Because these people are probably going to try to hire me to kill you," Clint said. "When they do I can identify them."

"To what end?"

"Arresting them."

"For what?"

"For trying to kill you." Clint was starting to feel exasperated with the young politician.

"But they won't try to kill me," Roosevelt said, "they'll try to hire you to do it. They can't be arrested for that. Not by a corrupt police department."

"What are you saying?"

"I'm saying," Roosevelt replied, "that we need them to make their attempt. Somebody has to try to kill me.

We have to stop that person and find out who hired him, and then we can have federal people come in and make the arrest, because some of the people arrested will surely be members of the police department, like Egan.''

Clint frowned. Roosevelt had a point, but did he want to take on the task of keeping the man alive?

"How about this?" Roosevelt asked, warming to his subject. "Nothing is going to happen until they approach you. When they do—and you turn them down—we'll have some idea of who's behind it. From that point on you become my bodyguard.''

"And who'll be mine?" Clint asked. "Because as soon as I turn them down, I'll become a target, as well."

"I told you," Roosevelt said, "I wear a pistol. I'll watch your back, and you watch mine.''

Clint had to think about that.

"I'm a dead shot," Roosevelt said. "I realize that you have had your back watched by the likes of Bat Masterson and Wyatt Earp, but I assure you, while I am not in their class, I can generally hit what I aim at.''

"Point," Clint said.

"Pardon me?''

"You don't aim a gun," Clint said, "you point it, as if it was an extension of one of your fingers.''

"Bully!" Teddy Roosevelt said. "In addition to keeping each other alive, I can learn some things from you. What do you say?''

Clint was unsure about placing his life in the hands of this brash young politician.

"Before you answer," Teddy said, "let me show you something. Come with me.''

Roosevelt quit the desk and hurried to the door. Clint was barely able to keep up with him. Roosevelt hurried down the hall to the stairway and led the way to the second floor. He hurried down a second floor hall, came to a closed door, and flung it open.

"Take a look," he said, allowing Clint to enter the room first.

Clint wasn't sure what he was looking at, for he'd never before seen a "gymnasium" as fully equipped as this one was. There were weights and other apparatus which he assumed were for exercise, and in the center of the room was what appeared to be a regulation boxing ring.

Roosevelt walked to the ring and picked a pair of gloves up from the apron.

"Would you like to go a few rounds? I've sparred with professionals."

"I don't think so, Teddy."

Roosevelt put the gloves back down and turned to face Clint.

"I was a sickly lad, Clint, frail and asthmatic. It took many hours of weight lifting and boxing to build myself into the man I am today. I still suffer from asthma occasionally, but for the most part I am as sound as a dollar. Now, if need be I can take you to a firing range and demonstrate my ability with a gun."

"We'll get to that, Teddy," Clint said. "Anybody who talks about 'aiming' a gun still has a lot to learn."

"That's fine, then," Roosevelt said. "I can't think of a better teacher than you, nor a better student than myself."

Roosevelt came closer to Clint, standing right in front of him. The politician was shorter, but packed more weight and probably more muscle. Clint didn't care if he never got into a boxing ring with the younger man.

"What do you say? You've brought me this information, and I am of the opinion that you are the only man for the job of keeping me alive. If you don't trust me to watch your back I understand. We can hire other men for that, but I want you to be in charge."

"We *would* need other men," Clint said, "because I'd have to sleep sometime—and it's not that I don't trust you, Teddy—"

Roosevelt held up his hand and said, "Say no more. Do this for me and I'll pay you handsomely."

"I'm not looking to be paid, Teddy," Clint said. "Like I said, once I turn these people down I'll be a target myself."

"Then it seems to me you have two choices," Teddy said.

"What are they?"

"Either take the job and kill me," Teddy said, "or keep me alive."

"All right, then," Clint said without hesitation. "You've got yourself a bodyguard."

"Bully!" young Roosevelt said, clasping Clint's hand in a viselike grip.

After Clint left the Roosevelt residence he realized that Teddy had so monopolized the conversation that he'd forgotten to tell the man about the attempt on his father. He'd have to bring that up the next time they talked. A family with two men in danger rather than one would need more than one bodyguard.

ELEVEN

This was the way they left it. Nothing had to be done until the offer to Clint was made. Clint only had to stay in his hotel and wait. Once the offer was made, and rejected, they decided that Clint would move into the Fifty-Seventh Street mansion to be close to Teddy. They would hire two other men who would work regular shifts, which would give Clint time to get some sleep.

Clint spent the next two days seeing more of what New York society had to offer, and eventually came to the conclusion that—except for Jane Evergreen—he had no use for the people who made up New York ''society.''

On the third day, after a strenuous—but glorious— night with Jane, Clint was once again having breakfast alone while she got her ''beauty sleep.''

"Uh-oh," Walter said, after pouring Clint a cup of coffee.

"What?"

"Look."

Clint saw Sergeant Egan approaching him once again, this time alone. Here it comes, he thought.

"It's all right, Walter," Clint said. "Go on about your business."

"Yes, sir."

"Hey, waiter," Egan called before Walter could leave.

Clint saw Walter swallow hard before he answered, "Yes, sir?" in a voice that was higher than his normal tone.

"Bring another coffee cup."

"Yes, sir."

Egan sat down opposite Clint without being invited. Under normal circumstances Clint would have extended an invitation for the man to leave. These were not, however, normal circumstances.

"I did some checking on you, Adams."

"Is that a fact?"

"Yeah, it is."

Egan seemed much more relaxed and arrogant without the other two men looking over his shoulder.

"And what did you find out?"

"Your reputation," Egan said. "I think it's made of paper."

"Come again?"

"You know," Egan said, "in the newspapers."

"Ah."

"I don't think you're much, you know?"

Clint sat back in his chair.

"Well, Sergeant," Clint said, "I've got much the same opinion of you."

That brought a murderous look from the man across the table.

"Careful how you talk to the law, Adams," Egan said. "You could get yourself in a lot of trouble."

"Egan," Clint said, "we both know you're here as a messenger boy, so deliver your message and let me finish my breakfast."

Egan's eyes narrowed and his hands flexed. Clint had the feeling that most of Egan's work was done with those big, ham-sized fists.

"Somebody wants to talk to you."

"Who?"

"That don't matter now," Egan said. He took a piece of paper out of his pocket. "Just be at this address at eight o'clock tonight, and don't have nobody with you."

"And who would I have with me?"

"Who knows?" Egan asked. "Maybe that little society piece you been playing with the past week or so."

Clint held his temper.

"Anything else?" he asked.

"No, that's it."

At that point Walter returned to the table carrying another coffee cup.

"That's all right, Walter," Clint said, "Sergeant Egan won't be needing that cup after all. He's leaving."

Egan glared across the table at Clint.

"You and me, Adams," he said, "we're gonna tangle before this is all over."

Clint chose not to reply at all, and after a few more moments Egan stood up and stalked out of the dining room.

"That's a dangerous man, Mr. Adams," Walter said. "He's crazy."

"That's okay, Walter," Clint said, "I've been known to go a little crazy a time or two myself."

TWELVE

The address on the piece of paper was a restaurant in Union Square on Fourteenth Street. Clint told Jane Evergreen only that he had to meet with someone and wouldn't be able to see her until later that night.

"It better not be a woman," she said teasingly.

"It's not," he said, although for all he knew, it might have been.

He entered the restaurant and was seated at a table. Nothing had been said about how he would recognize anyone, so he assumed he would be approached. He decided to order dinner while he was waiting. He requested a steak, potatoes, and other vegetables, and beer, and ate at a leisurely pace. It was nine p.m. and he was considering what kind of pie to have when a man entered and came straight for him.

"Clint Adams?"

"That's right."

The man sat down.

"My name is not important."

The man was tall, slender, hawk-nosed, and well hidden beneath a black cape and a broad-brimmed fedora.

"It is if you want to talk to me," Clint said. "I'm not here to play games."

The man opposite him sat in silence, then Clint heard a sigh and the fedora was removed. The man's eyes were feral, like the eyes of a rat, and were even tinged with yellow, although the irises were brown. His black hair came to a widow's peak, and his face was pale, almost colorless, as were his lips.

"My name," he said, "is Lamont."

"Is that your first or last name?"

"It's my name," the man said. "Take it or leave it."

"What's on your mind, Mr. Lamont?" Clint said, deciding to treat the name as the man's last.

"It is my understanding that you hire out your gun."

"Then you're misinformed."

The man frowned.

"I don't understand."

"Obviously."

Now the man seemed annoyed. He looked around, as if he suspected he had been lured here under false pretenses.

"I don't like to play games either, Adams," he finally said. "I understood that you were approached about hiring out, and that it all depended on the price."

"And the job."

"The job is murder," Lamont said plainly. "I'm sure that's not something you're unfamiliar with. You've killed men before."

"Never for money."

"This would be for a lot of money."

"How much?"

Lamont named a figure. He was right. It *was* a lot of money. Once Clint turned this offer down it wouldn't be hard for Lamont, and the people he worked for, to find someone else.

"And who is the target?" Clint asked.

"Theodore Roosevelt."

"Senior or Junior?"

That was when the surprise came.

"Senior."

"What?"

"I said Senior."

Clint frowned.

"Are you sure?"

"Of course I'm sure," Lamont said. "I'm doing the hiring, ain't I?"

"Theodore Roosevelt . . . Senior?"

"Why is that so hard to believe?"

"Well, Teddy Roosevelt is a politician," Clint said. "I would think he'd be the Roosevelt—"

"The father is a wealthy man," Lamont said, "with his fingers in a lot of pies."

"And somebody wants his fingers out of a certain pie?" Clint asked.

"Permanently."

Clint wondered how to play this, now that the target had changed. He finally decided to go ahead with his plan of turning down the offer. Moving into the mansion would still be a viable plan.

"Well?" Lamont said. "Do you want the job?"

"No."

"Why not?"

"I don't hire out."

Lamont hesitated a moment, then said, "We'll raise the price."

"No," Clint said.

Lamont named a figure.

"Not at any price."

Lamont looked around again suspiciously.

"There's nobody else here," Clint said. "Just you and me."

"Why did you come?"

"To listen to an offer."

"But—" Lamont stopped short.

"But what?"

Abruptly, the man replaced his hat, drew it down over his eyes.

"You'll be sorry," he said.

"For what?"

But Lamont didn't answer. He stood, turned, and hurried from the restaurant. If he was looking to go unnoticed, Clint thought, he should have forgotten about the cape. It swirled as he moved, and almost got caught in the door behind him. It was almost as though the man was wearing a costume, although it was a far cry from Halloween.

"Have you decided on your pie, sir?" the waiter asked.

"Yes," Clint said, "I'll have pumpkin."

THIRTEEN

Clint had to settle for peach pie. Of course he knew the place wouldn't have pumpkin pie, but the man, Lamont, had put him in mind of Halloween, with his fedora and cape. He wondered if Teddy Roosevelt would know who the man was.

He finished his pie and coffee, and walked to the front door. Instinct told him not to step outside immediately. It saved his life. He opened the door and paused long enough so that the first shot missed by a wide margin. Whoever the shooter was, he was impatient. Clint had been right when he'd told Roosevelt that turning this job down would make a target of him, but he didn't know that it would happen this fast.

Clint reacted immediately. He threw himself out the door, drew his gun, and rolled on the ground until he came to a stop beyond one of the trees that lined the street. It was a small tree and did not afford much cover, but it was dark out and he doubted the shooter would be able to find him. Although the streetlamps were lit, they did not supply enough light to assist the shooter in locating his target.

He remained where he was until he distinctly heard the sound of footsteps running away. Apparently, the shooter was satisfied to have made one attempt. He stood up and holstered his gun. He decided to go directly to the Roosevelt home on Fifty-Seventh Street, and started looking for a cab to take him there.

This time the door was answered by a butler, who showed Clint into the den rather than the study. There was no desk here, but the walls were lined with books. Clint waited ten minutes until Teddy came down, wearing a ridiculous-looking sleeping gown.

"Never mind what I sleep in," Teddy said, seeing the look on Clint's face, "what brings you here so late?"

"Well, first off I didn't think it was that late," Clint said.

"I have early meetings in the morning," Roosevelt said, "or it wouldn't be."

"The offer was made to me tonight."

This news excited Roosevelt.

"That's excellent," he said. "How much did they offer?"

Clint named the figure that was quoted to him.

"Is that all?"

"It was raised when I turned down the first offer."

"All right," Roosevelt said. "Who made the offer?"

"A man named Lamont. Do you know him?"

"Not by name. Describe him."

Clint did, and Roosevelt listened intently.

"Know him now?"

"If I'd seen such a man I'd remember," Teddy said. "This is bad. I thought we'd be able to tell where the offer was coming from, which of my enemies was—"

"None."

"I beg your pardon?"

"It's none of your enemies."

"Why do you say that?"

"Because they didn't try to hire me to kill you, Teddy."

"I'm confused."

"They tried to hire me to kill your father," Clint said. "The offer was to kill Theodore Roosevelt, Senior."

Teddy frowned.

"Now I am confused."

Hurriedly, he turned and closed the twin doors to the den.

"Tell me again of this meeting."

Clint recounted the incidents of the evening once again, this time adding the fact that he was shot at while leaving the restaurant.

"I know the restaurant," Roosevelt said. "It doesn't help us, because I know the owner is not involved in anything dastardly."

"Dastardly" was a word Clint knew, but he'd never heard anyone use it before.

"This fellow Lamont, that doesn't help us, either," Teddy said.

"What about the fact that the intended victim is your father?" Clint asked.

"That doesn't help," Teddy said. "He has more enemies than I do."

"Don't I know it."

"What do you mean?"

"There's more," Clint said, and told Teddy what had happened after the Brooklyn Bridge ceremony.

"Well," Teddy said when Clint was finished, "it seems you've already done my family a great service, Clint."

"Shouldn't we awaken him and tell him what's happened?" Clint asked.

"Not yet," Teddy said. "I want to think about this for a while. Actually, it doesn't change our plans very much. You can still move in here starting tomorrow—that is, if you will undertake the assignment of being my father's bodyguard?"

"Of course."

"Thank you. I will still assist you, and we can still bring in two other men."

"Why would you not want to tell your father about it?" Clint asked.

"He's a proud man, Clint," Teddy said. "This would not frighten him, and I do not believe he would accept a bodyguard."

"What do you want to do, then?"

"I think we should let him believe that you are here to guard me," Teddy said. "He would then accept your presence in the house. Is that all right with you?"

"It's fine, Teddy," Clint said. "However you want to handle it."

"Good," he said. "Don't even check out of your hotel in the morning, just come here and be prepared to stay. I'll supply you with anything you might need, like clothes and weapons and such."

It was a good idea not to tip anyone off by actually checking out of the hotel.

"I'll be here, and I'll have my own guns."

"And you have my apologies," Teddy said, opening the den doors.

"For what?"

"For taking you away from Miss Jane Evergreen for as long as this will take."

"Oh," Clint said, "I forgot about that. Well, I'm sure Jane will understand."

"What will you tell her?"

"As little as I can, without getting her mad at me."

"Sound idea," Teddy said, slapping Clint on the back. "Come on, I'll let you out."

When they got to the door Teddy opened it and said, "I can't tell you how much I appreciate your help, Clint. Without you my father's life probably would have been forfeit."

"I'm glad to help, Teddy," Clint said.

"I'm also honored to be working by your side," Teddy said. "I don't mind telling you I'm excited by all of this."

"A little excitement is fine," Clint said, "as long as it's not the death of us."

FOURTEEN

Lamont entered his boss's office and stood before his desk.

"What are you dressed up for?" the man asked.

"I didn't want to be recognized."

"Take off that ridiculous getup."

Lamont removed his fedora and cape and set them aside on a chair.

"What happened?"

"He turned down the offer."

"What?" The man behind the desk was obviously surprised. "I thought it was just a matter of price."

"I raised the price and he still refused."

"What kind of a game is this?" the other man asked. "Were you seen?"

"I doubt it," Lamont said. "I checked around, but it looked like he was there alone."

"Why was he there if he wasn't going to take the job?"

"That's what I was wondering."

"He's dangerous now."

"I know."

"He'll have to be dealt with."

"Yes."

Lamont didn't bother telling his boss that he had tried and missed.

"We'll have to move fast," the man behind the desk said. "Do we have some other men in mind for the job?"

"Yes," Lamont said.

"Good. Bring them to me in the morning so I can talk to them. We'll have two targets for them now."

"Yes, sir."

"This time it better not be botched," the man behind the desk said. "It'll be on your head."

"The last time wasn't my fault," Lamont said. "Somebody interf—"

"Don't whine, Lamont."

Lamont reached for his hat and cape.

"And don't put those things on again!"

"Yes, sir."

FIFTEEN

Clint spent the night with Jane and in the morning explained that he would be doing some work over the next few days that would keep him from seeing her.

"That will bring you very close to the day you were intending to leave New York," she said, lying quietly in bed beside him.

"Yes, it will." He had only intended to stay ten days to two weeks.

"Will I see you again before you leave?"

"Yes, of course you will."

"Because if you didn't want to see me anymore all you would have to do is say so."

"No, that's not it at all, Jane," he said. "Through no fault of my own I've gotten myself involved with something that I have to see through. I swear that it has nothing to do with you and me."

She smiled and said, "I believe you. I suspect it's time for me to go home, anyway."

"To Brooklyn?"

She nodded. She had told him when they first met that she lived in Brooklyn, in an area called Brooklyn Heights.

"I'll be there, then, when you're ready to see me again," she said. "You have the address in your room."

"Yes, I do."

"Will you be checking out of the hotel?"

"No, I'll be keeping my room."

She put her arms out to him.

"Make love to me now, Clint, in a way that will stay with me until I see you again."

Clint was sorry that he was unable to tell her what was really going on, but the truth was he couldn't trust her not to tell some of her society friends, and then the information might find its way into the newspaper.

But making love to her so that she'd remember, that was something he definitely could do.

He left the hotel that morning, leaving behind all of his belongings except his guns. When he got to the Roosevelt house Teddy was waiting for him.

"I'll show you to your room," he said. "My father is out for the day, and I convinced my mother to go to Oyster Bay to be with Alice."

"How did you do that without telling her what was going on?"

"I didn't," Teddy said. "That is, I *did* tell her what was going on. My mother is a strong, sensible woman, Clint. She knew why I was keeping this from my father,

and she knows that I will do whatever it takes to keep
him safe.''

Teddy showed Clint to a room that was more sumptuous than the hotel room in the Biltmore.

''All of the house staff know you're going to be here.
They think you're simply a guest, but they also know
that you have the run of the house.''

''All right,'' Clint said, still admiring the room.

''There are clothes in the chest of drawers, there, and
in the closet.''

Clint looked in both places and found more clothing
than he'd ever wear, and in his size.

''How'd you know my size?''

Teddy shrugged and said, ''Good guess.''

''What about the other two men?''

''I've got six men coming in today, starting at noon,''
Teddy said. ''You interview them and hire the two you
want. I'll pay them what you think they're worth.''

''Okay.''

''I have some questions, Clint,'' Teddy said. ''Let's
go down to the study.''

Clint followed Teddy back downstairs and felt comfortable that he knew his way to and from his room.
He'd prowl the house on his own later on.

In the study Teddy sat behind the desk, and Clint sat
in a chair across from him.

''What are your questions?''

''I guess the most important one is, how long can you
stay?''

''That's a good question. Given the amount of money
that was tossed at me last night I don't think it will be
too long before they find someone who will take it. I
don't anticipate I'll have to be here more than a week

or so. If they don't try by then, I might have to find someone else to come in and help you. I can recommend two of three reliable men who can come in from out of town—''

"Let's not talk about that right now," Teddy said. "Let's wait until the week is up."

"All right. Any other questions?"

"There will be," Teddy said. "I'm still collecting my thoughts."

"Then I'll ask you one," Clint said. "These six men you're bringing in to be interviewed. How much can you trust them?"

Teddy shrugged and said, "They're for hire, like anyone else. For all I know they've also been approached. There's one, though, who comes highly recommended. He's coming in at noon."

"Who is he?"

"His name is Delvecchio. I understand he's a detective as well as a bodyguard. He's done some work for some of my colleagues. He lives in Brooklyn."

"Good," Clint said, "we'll need an experienced man. When will your father be back?"

"Late this evening."

"Where is he?"

"He's down on Wall Street, at his office. He should be safe there."

"I hope that's true," Clint said. "Maybe we can send this Delvecchio down there to watch him."

"Already planning to hire him?"

"If what you say is true, and if I like him," Clint said, "yes. What about the other five?"

"Just men for hire."

"Maybe Delvecchio will have a suggestion."

"Perhaps he will."

"Let's go over your routine, and your father's," Clint said. "I want to know what each of you do from the moment you get up in the morning—which is when?"

"We'll both be up by eight a.m., most likely . . ." Roosevelt began, and proceeded to run through his and his father's day with Clint, who listened intently.

"How do you intend to work this with my father?" Teddy asked. "You can't stay with him without arousing some suspicion."

"I thought I'd tell him that I need him to stay close to you, for your safety."

Teddy smiled.

"That might work, but he and I don't work in the same circles," the young politician said. "He's not going to come to assembly meetings with me."

"Then I might simply have to stay with him during the day without his knowledge. The evenings will be easier, since you and I will both be in the house."

"And when you're asleep?"

"The two men we hire will alternate watching the house from outside."

"It's too bad some of your colleagues are not in town," Teddy said. "Having someone like Wyatt Earp here, or Talbot Roper, would be . . ."

"Exciting?"

"Well . . . yes," Teddy said, almost sheepishly.

"Teddy," Clint said, "don't get so excited that you forget what we're doing here."

"Clint," Roosevelt said, "I can assure you that I will not forget that we are working together to save my father's life."

"No," Clint said, "of course not. I apologize."

"Don't," Teddy said. "The one thing you'll always be able to do with me is speak your mind. And now I have another matter."

"Which is?"

"Pool," Teddy said. "I suggest we shoot a game while we're waiting for Mr. Delvecchio to arrive."

"A dollar a ball?" Clint asked.

"Well," Teddy said, "you do owe me a chance to get even."

SIXTEEN

Frank Kenrick was getting tired of cooling his heels, but this job promised to pay so much he decided not to complain.

"When are we gonna get in?" Pete Haney said, sitting next to Kenrick in the waiting room. "And why did we have to wear these suits?"

"We have to blend in, stupid," Kenrick said. "Stop complaining."

"But—"

"But nothing," Kenrick said, cutting him off. "You know how much this job promises to pay. I'm not gonna blow this job because you're impatient. If you wanna leave, I can handle it myself."

"How do you know that?" Haney asked. "We don't even know what the job is."

"We know that it pays big," Kenrick said. "That's all I have to know. Now shut up."

Finally, a door opened and the man they knew as Lamont came out.

"Come this way, gentlemen," he said. "It's time."

As they got up Kenrick said to Haney, "Just let me do the talking."

"Yeah, yeah . . ."

The man behind the desk regarded the two men critically. Both looked grossly overdressed and uncomfortable, and one of them looked like an idiot.

"Which one of you is Kenrick?" he asked.

"I am."

Good. It wasn't the one who looked like an idiot.

"What's your name?" he asked the other man.

"Haney."

"You can wait outside."

"But—"

"I want to talk to Mr. Kenrick alone."

"But—"

"Wait outside," Kenrick said. Haney shut his mouth and left the room.

"Have a seat."

Kenrick sat. He noticed that the man did not offer him a drink, even though there was a bar in the room.

"Does he do everything you tell him?" the man behind the desk asked.

"Everything."

"Without question?"

"Without question."

"Why?"

"Because he knows he stands to make more money

with me than without me, and either I run the show or we split up.''

''Do you need him?''

Kenrick seemed to think that question over for a few moments.

''Need is a strong word,'' he finally said. ''I do better with him. The extra eyes and hands come in handy.''

''Then if I hire one of you, I hire both?''

''That's right.''

''For one price?''

''The going rate.''

''Which is?''

''Whatever you're offering for this job.''

''What have you heard about this job?''

''Only that it will pay a lot.''

''That's true. You don't know who the target is?''

''No.''

''Do you care?''

''No.''

''What if there were two targets?''

''At double the price?''

The man hedged.

''The second would be slightly cheaper than the first,'' he replied. ''He's an annoyance.''

''Then we can negotiate.''

''You have a certain reputation in New York, Mr. Kenrick,'' the man said. ''You come highly recommended.''

''That's nice to know.''

''I hope you can live up to your reputation.''

''Reputations are always kind of exaggerated,'' Kenrick said.

''For your sake, I hope that's true.''

"Come again?"

"The second man we were talking about? The annoyance?"

"What about him?"

"He has something of a reputation, too," the man said. "But he's in my way and I need him removed."

"And who might this fella be?"

"Clint Adams."

It was obvious that Kenrick recognized the name immediately.

"Ah, you know of him."

"Of course," Kenrick said, trying to keep his voice steady. His heart was beating with excitement. He didn't want to give away to this man—the man with the money—that he would go after the Gunsmith for free. "Everybody who's ever made his way with a gun knows the Gunsmith."

"And you will still take this job even though he is involved?"

"Are you still paying top dollar?"

"I am."

"Then there's no question that I'm taking the job."

"And your . . . partner?"

"I speak for him, too."

"Good," the moneyman said, "then let's get down to business."

SEVENTEEN

When Delvecchio arrived he was shown into the study, where Clint was sitting behind the desk. Teddy Roosevelt had decided that Clint should conduct these interviews without him.

"Oh," Delvecchio said, "I thought I'd be seeing Mr. Roosevelt—uh, Junior."

"My name's Clint Adams. If you take this job you'll be getting paid by Mr. Roosevelt, Junior, but you'll actually be working for me."

The man came forward and shook hands with Clint, who studied him closely. He was of average height, in his thirties, and fit-looking.

"This isn't a joke, right?" he asked.

"What isn't?"

"You're Clint Adams?"

"That's right."

77

"The same Clint Adams who was at the Brooklyn Bridge opening?"

"Yes."

"The same . . . you're the Gunsmith, right?"

"I have been called that," Clint said, "yes."

"Well . . ."

"Have a seat, Mr. Delvecchio."

The man sat where Clint had been sitting when Teddy was behind the desk.

"Is there some reason you wouldn't want this job because of who I am?" Clint asked.

"Oh, hell, no," Delvecchio said. "I just never thought I'd ever get a chance to meet someone like you . . . uh, I mean, you know, a legend from the, uh, old West."

"The not-so-old West," Clint said, "but I know what you mean. Do me a favor and don't believe half of what you've read, and half of what you've heard, and we should get along okay."

"That's fine with me," Delvecchio said. "So what's the job?"

"We have to keep Theodore Roosevelt, Senior, alive."

"Have threats been made?"

"Not exactly," Clint said.

"Then maybe you should tell me what we're talking about . . . exactly."

Briefly, Clint explained how he had been approached with the job of killing Theodore Roosevelt, Senior, and what he had done about it.

"How long does this job figure to be?" Delvecchio asked.

"Until the attempt has been made."

"And will there only be one attempt?"

"If we stop the first and find out who was behind it, yes."

"How much is being offered?"

"I can tell you how much was offered to me," Clint said and named the amount.

Delvecchio whistled.

"With that kind of money being offered I'm surprised I haven't heard anything on the street."

"Don't you live in Brooklyn?"

"I do, but I also work in Manhattan. If that much money is on the street, I should hear about it."

"Are your contacts that good?"

"They are."

"Well," Clint said, "the offer was only made to me last night. It might not, uh, hit the streets until today."

"I'll keep my ears open."

"You wouldn't be interested in that kind of an offer, would you?" Clint asked.

He thought Delvecchio might get insulted, but the man was calm.

"It's not my kind of job," he said.

"Well," Clint said, "this job is yours, if you want it."

"I do," Delvecchio said. "How much does it pay?"

Clint told him the price that he and Roosevelt had agreed on.

"That's good money. How many other men are you hiring on?"

"Just one."

"And who might that be?"

"Somebody from this list," Clint said, handing him the list Roosevelt had made.

Delvecchio scanned it and handed it back.

"What do you think?" Clint asked.

"Who made that list?"

"Teddy Roosevelt."

"There are at least two names there who might take the job from the other side. Inviting them into this house might make it easier for them."

Clint handed the list back. He liked Delvecchio and thought he could trust the man's judgment.

"Cross their names off."

Delvecchio did.

"What about the others?"

"I know them all," Delvecchio said. "If you want my recommendation, hire the third name on the list."

Clint looked at the name.

"Anson Eickhorst?"

Delvecchio nodded.

"What kind of man is he?"

"He's a lawyer, but he hasn't practiced law for a while."

"Why not?"

"It'd be up to him to tell you. All I can tell you is that he's a good man with a gun, if you can keep him away from the women long enough—or them away from him. He's quite a ladies' man."

"Can I trust him if I hire him?"

Delvecchio nodded.

"He'll do whatever it takes to get the job done."

"Okay, then," Clint said, putting the list down on the table. "He's scheduled for a five o'clock interview. Can you get him here before then?"

"I can."

"Do it, then," Clint said. "Can you both be back here, say, three?"

Delvecchio nodded.

"Good. When you both get here I'll tell you what your jobs are."

"I assume you're taking the inside of the house?"

"That's right."

"Then I guess we'll have the outside."

"Right."

Delvecchio nodded and stood up.

"Any more questions?" Clint asked.

"If I have any more," Delvecchio said, "I'll ask them at three o'clock."

The two men shook hands and Delvecchio left, promising to be back by three, with Eickhorst.

It was only several moments after the door closed on Delvecchio that Teddy Roosevelt appeared.

"How did it go?"

"Real well," Clint said. "I like him. He'll be a good man to have."

"And for a second man?"

"He recommended one of the men on your list, and will be back with him at three."

"We're all set, then," Roosevelt said.

"At three o'clock we'll give them their assignments," Clint said.

"Which will be?" Teddy asked.

"Close the door," Clint said, "and we'll figure that out right now."

EIGHTEEN

Haney listened intently while Kenrick explained what their job was. They were celebrating in a saloon near the office of the man who had just hired them.

"Wait a minute," Haney said.

"What?"

"I may be slow, but I ain't stupid, Kenrick."

"What do you mean?"

"You keep sayin' that we'll be takin' care of this second man, but you ain't sayin' who the second man is. Why is that?"

"Don't be silly," Kenrick said. "I'll tell you who the second man is."

"Then go ahead," Haney said. "Tell me."

"His name's Clint Adams."

Haney stared at him.

"He's also known as—"

"I *know* who the Gunsmith is, Kenrick!" Haney said, interrupting him. "Are we gettin' paid enough to go up against him?"

Kenrick named the figure they were being paid, and Haney's eyes bugged.

"Each?"

"No," Kenrick said, "together."

"That's still a lot of money."

"It certainly is."

"Yeah, but you got to be alive to spend it."

"Well, I tell you what," Kenrick said. "We'll split this job up. What do you say?"

"Split it up how?" Haney asked suspiciously.

"You take the banker," Kenrick said, "and I'll take the Gunsmith."

"You want him that bad?"

"You know how famous the man who kills the Gunsmith is going to be?" Kenrick asked. "Like Jack McCall."

"Who?"

"McCall," Kenrick said, annoyed. "He's the man who killed Wild Bill Hickok."

Haney frowned.

"Didn't he shoot Hickok in the back?"

"What's the difference?" Kenrick asked. "He killed him, didn't he? Like Robert Ford."

"Who?"

"He killed Jesse James last year!"

"Didn't he shoot Jesse in the back?"

Now Kenrick was getting angry. Haney was missing the point.

"I wouldn't want to be known as a back-shooter,"

Haney went on. "You gonna shoot the Gunsmith in the back?"

"You worry about killing the banker," Kenrick said, "and I'll worry about Clint Adams. Okay?"

"Okay."

"Fine," Kenrick said.

A moment passed while the two men sipped beer from their mugs and then Haney said, "I ain't shootin' the banker in the back, though."

NINETEEN

When Delvecchio returned at three he had a white-haired man with him. The man's age was hard to figure, as he was tall and fit and moved well. The white hair might have been premature, but it was hard to say. That really didn't matter, though, as long as he could do the job.

The thing Clint found odd was that while Delvecchio told him that Eickhorst was a lawyer who, for some reason, did not practice, the man was dressed in a three-piece suit, as if he were ready to go into court at any time. He also had a gun in a shoulder holster beneath the jacket and—Clint could tell—either another gun or a knife in his right boot.

They were in the study again, and this time Teddy Roosevelt was present.

''Mr. Roosevelt and I will see to his father's safety

while inside the house,'' Clint said, while Teddy looked on. ''You will each take four-hour shifts outside the house, so we can get some sleep.''

''And what about when he's away from the house?'' Eickhorst asked.

''We'll split that duty, as well,'' Clint said. ''Two of us will have that duty at all times.''

''We'll draw up a chart,'' Teddy said, ''and we'll all have a copy.''

''I have a question,'' Eickhorst said.

''What is it?'' Clint asked.

''Well, actually it's a comment,'' the man said. ''I don't think Mr. Roosevelt, here, should be part of this team.''

Teddy bristled and stood up straight.

''And why not?''

''Excuse me, sir,'' Eickhorst said to Teddy, who had to be anywhere from ten to fifteen years younger, ''but you're not a professional.''

''I can vouch for Mr. Roosevelt's fitness for this job,'' Clint said.

''Well, if *you'll* excuse me, Mr. Adams, I don't really know what your qualifications are, either.''

Clint exchanged a glance with Delvecchio, who simply shrugged. He did not have anything to do with what Eickhorst was saying.

''Mr. Eickhorst,'' Clint said, ''I think all you'll have to keep in mind is that we are paying you.''

''I like to know I've got someone who knows what they're doing watching my back,'' Eickhorst said.

''I guess you'll have to count on a little bit of adventure to go with the money you're being paid,'' Clint said, and then added, ''which is very good money.''

"Yes, it is," Eickhorst said. "The money is, indeed, excellent."

"Then are there any more questions or comments?" Clint asked.

Delvecchio shook his head, and Eickhorst simply did not respond.

"Mr. Roosevelt is at his office on Wall Street," Clint said. "Delvecchio, I'd like you and . . . can I call you Anson?" he asked the other man.

"Please do."

"And . . . do you have a first name?" Clint asked Delvecchio.

"Delvecchio will do," the other man said, "or Del, if you wish."

"Whatever I call you," Clint said, "I'd like the two of you to go to Wall Street now and stay with Mr. Roosevelt until he arrives home. Once he's in the house, you two can decide who will take the midnight-to-four shift, and who will watch the house from four to eight."

"At eight," Roosevelt said, taking up the narrative, "whichever of you is on duty will come to the back door. If there are any special instructions, or if you have anything to report, that's when we will make the exchange."

"Is this all understood?" Clint asked.

"Yes," Delvecchio said.

"Understood," Eickhorst said.

"Good. Get going."

Both men headed for the door, and then Eickhorst turned back.

"Yes?" Clint asked.

"In the event that contact is made," he said, "what are our instructions?"

"Keep my father alive," Roosevelt said.

"At any cost?" Eickhorst asked.

"You heard the man," Clint said. "You will keep Theodore Roosevelt, Senior, alive . . . period."

TWENTY

At 8:35 p.m. Theodore Roosevelt, Senior, entered the Roosevelt home on West Fifty-Seventh Street.

Clint and Teddy were playing pool when the house-man stuck his head in the door.

"Mr. Roosevelt, Senior, is home, sir."

"Thank you, Charles," Teddy said. "How much do I owe you now?" he asked Clint.

"Five hundred and three dollars," Clint said.

"Can we just keep the game going?"

"Indefinitely," Clint said, "or until you run out of money."

They replaced their sticks in the rack on the wall.

"Are you sure you haven't played this game much before?" Teddy asked.

"Positive."

"You have amazing hand-to-eye coordination. I won-

91

der what kind of a baseball player you would have been."

Clint shrugged and decided not to tell Teddy that he'd spent one year—or baseball "season"—pitching for a professional team.

They went downstairs and met with Teddy's father, who immediately inquired as to where his wife was.

"She went out to Oyster Bay, Father," Teddy said. "Alice needed some help with, uh, something."

Clint immediately recognized that, unlike most politicians of the day—or of any day—Teddy Roosevelt appeared to be a very poor liar—at least, where his father was concerned.

"Uh-huh," the senior Roosevelt said. He then looked at Clint. "And I assume that you are our houseguest, Clint Adams?"

"That's right, sir," Clint said, immediately stepping forward and extending his hand. "We met briefly before."

Roosevelt, Sr., accepted it and punished it briefly, then released it.

"I know that, sir. I am not a fool. And as our houseguest, are you as prepared to lie to my face as my son appears to be?"

"Father—"

"First," Roosevelt, Sr., said to his son, "I see two hoodlums following me all over Manhattan as of four o'clock this afternoon, and then I arrive home and you tell me a whopper about your wife needing your mother in Oyster Bay, when I know your wife to be perfectly capable of handling any situation all by her lonesome."

"It was, uh, a question of, uh, a decorating thing," Teddy stammered.

"Nonsense!" Roosevelt, Sr., turned his accusing gaze on Clint.

"Teddy," Clint said. "I believe your father needs to know the truth."

"That," Roosevelt, Sr., said, "would be refreshing."

"Uh, Father, if we could all go into the den and have a drink, I'll explain."

"And about time, too," Roosevelt said and led the way.

When they each had a brandy in hand Teddy told his father what Clint had discovered, and what they had done since that time.

"So those hoodlums who were following me—"

"—were not hoodlums, at all. They were keeping you safe from harm."

"As if I needed two street toughs to keep me safe," Roosevelt, Sr., scoffed.

"They're very capable men, Father," Teddy said.

"I'm sure they are," the older man said, "but I don't want them following me."

"I'm afraid you don't have a choice in the matter," Teddy said. "I'm paying them to protect you, until the attempt on your life is made and we can find out who's behind it."

"And you?" the senior Roosevelt asked Clint. "Are you getting paid, too?"

"No, sir," Clint said. "I haven't asked for any money. I just want to keep you safe."

At that point Teddy told his father how Clint had saved his life at the bridge ceremony. Theodore Roosevelt, Sr., stared into his glass, then finished off his brandy and set the glass down on the desk.

"I guess I can't fault either of you for your motives," he said, "and I thank you, sir, for what you've already done." He took a deep breath. "All right, then, I'll co-operate. I take it you haven't gone to the police?"

"No," Teddy said.

"That's just as well," Theodore said. "They're a corrupt lot."

"There must be a policeman you think is honest," Clint said.

The two Roosevelts exchanged a glance.

"I met some police the last time I was here," Clint said.

"When was that?" Teddy asked.

"A few years—"

"Forget it," Theodore said. "There's been a turnover of personnel two or three times since then. No, right now the New York City Police Department is riddled with corruption. It's one of the things Teddy is trying to do something about."

"Then why isn't he a target?" Clint asked.

"I don't know," Theodore said. "Tell me again, Clint, about the man who tried to hire you."

"He said his name was Lamont." Clint described the man to him.

"Why would he give you his name?" Theodore asked.

"I don't know," Clint said. "I guess they felt pretty safe in assuming I was going to take the job."

"And the policeman? You say his name is Egan?"

"That's right," Clint said. "Sergeant Egan."

Theodore looked at his son.

"Maybe we can find out who Egan is working for, Teddy," he said.

Teddy found himself feeling grateful that his father did not use his childhood nickname, "Teedie," in front of Clint. It was an odd thing to think of at that moment.

"Well, between us we know a lot of people," he replied. "Maybe somebody will know something."

"Meanwhile," Clint said, "we'll go on with our plan."

"Which is?" Theodore asked.

"To keep you alive, sir."

Theodore stuck his finger inside his collar, as if to loosen it, and said, "Well, at least you have a good plan."

TWENTY-ONE

At eight-thirty the next morning Clint was in the kitchen with the cook—a black man named Elias who had spent his entire life in the Northeast and did not know anything of slavery—when there was a knock at the back door.

"I'll get it, Elias," Clint said.

"As you wish, sir. Will there be another for breakfast, sir?"

Clint's first instinct was to say no, but since Theodore, Sr., knew everything now, maybe he should also meet the other men who were working to keep him safe.

"Yes, Elias, there will be."

"Very good, sir."

Clint went and opened the door and saw Delvecchio standing out there.

"I got the four to eight shift," Delvecchio said, yawning. "Is there anything we need to talk about?"

"I think so," Clint said. "Come on in."

Delvecchio entered the kitchen, and Clint closed the door behind him.

"This is bigger than the room I live in," Delvecchio said.

"Where's that?"

"A rooming house on Sackett Street."

"Take off your jacket," Clint said. "You're staying for breakfast."

Delvecchio sniffed the air and said, "I'm not gonna argue with you."

"First off, Mr. Roosevelt knows everything."

"Senior?"

Clint nodded.

"He spotted us?"

"Yes," Clint said, "both of you."

"Damn," Delvecchio said, frowning and looking for someplace to put his jacket. "That doesn't speak very well of my abilities, does it?"

"I think we're dealing with an extraordinary man, here, Delvecchio, so I wouldn't let that bother you. By the way, did you see anything out there this morning?"

"No, nothing," Delvecchio said, finally putting his jacket on the back of a chair for want of somewhere better. "And Anson didn't see anything, either."

"Okay," Clint said. "The plan's the same, even though Mr. Roosevelt will know you're there now."

"This is Senior, right?"

"Let's get this straight," Clint said. "Mr. Roosevelt is Senior. When I mean Junior, I'll say Teddy."

"Got it."

"I figure you'll have breakfast with us this morning

and meet him. Anson can do the same thing tomorrow morning, if he wants.''

''I don't think he will.''

''Why not?''

''He's sort of antisocial,'' Delvecchio said. ''Also, I don't think he wants to get to know Mr. Roosevelt personally, you know, just in case we, uh, don't do our job.''

''I see,'' Clint said. ''Well, I guess that makes some kind of sense. Come on, let's go into the dining room.''

When they got there Teddy was already seated and drinking a cup of coffee. He frowned as Clint entered with Delvecchio.

''I thought your father should meet him, since he's agreed to go along with our plan.''

''Good idea,'' Teddy said. ''Have a seat, Mr. Delvecchio.''

''Thank you.''

''You look tired.''

''I'm not, really,'' Delvecchio said. ''I slept until two, and then walked across the Brooklyn Bridge before catching a cab.''

''Ah,'' Teddy said, his eyes lighting up, ''what was that like?''

''It was . . . odd,'' Delvecchio said, as Clint seated himself across from him. Teddy sat at the foot of the table, leaving the head of the table for his father. ''I enjoyed it, though. I understand people are walking across both ways during the days. When I did it there was no one else in sight.''

''It sounds like an experience I should try,'' Teddy said.

''I recommend it.''

"What are you recommending?"

They all turned at the sound of Theodore Senior's voice. He was wearing one of his banker's three-piece suits, and Clint found it odd that Anson Eickhorst had been wearing one just like it yesterday.

"A walk across the Brooklyn Bridge, sir," Delvecchio said.

"I understand you are one of my bodyguards," Roosevelt said.

"Yes, sir."

The older man walked over to Delvecchio and held out his hand.

"Delvecchio is my name, sir," Delvecchio said, shaking hands firmly.

"Glad to meet you, Mr. Delvecchio. Are you good at your job?"

"I thought so, sir."

Theodore took his seat and asked, "What changed your mind, sir?"

"You did," Delvecchio said. "I understand you spotted me yesterday."

"Don't take that too hard," Roosevelt said. "You didn't belong on Wall Street. Neither did your partner."

"He was wearing a suit very much like yours . . . . sir," Delvecchio said.

"Nevertheless," Roosevelt said, "he did not belong on Wall Street, either."

"I guess not."

Elias came in with breakfast, which consisted of ham, eggs, potatoes, pancakes, biscuits—with butter or honey—and, for anyone who wanted it, steak.

Everybody wanted it, because they all fell quiet and attacked the food.

TWENTY-TWO

Conversation did not begin again until the food was finished and everyone had a last cup of coffee in front of them.

"I think I'm about to bust," Delvecchio said.

"You don't know?" Clint asked.

"I've never been this full before," the man answered. "I'm afraid I don't know my bursting point."

"Well, I do," Clint said, "and I'm not far from it. Teddy, I may stay a lot longer than I planned."

"Stay as long as you like," Teddy said.

"Isn't that just like a boy?" Theodore commented. "Invite his friends to stay, and then he'll go off to Oyster Bay with his wife."

Clint assumed that Mr. Roosevelt was kidding.

"Well," Theodore said, looking around the table, "who's coming to work with me today?"

"I'm afraid I am, sir," Delvecchio said. "Anson will be relieving me about noon."

"Ah, just in time for lunch," the elder Roosevelt said. "Perhaps I'll be able to find his bursting point. I just have to get some papers, Mr. Delvecchio, and then we'll be off."

"I'll be ready, sir."

The three men remained silent until Theodore, Sr., had left the room.

"You might have to start dressing better if he's going to start taking you to lunch," Teddy said to Delvecchio.

"I think I'll leave the lunches to Anson," Delvecchio said. "He's always dressed for the part."

"Yes, I understand you said Mr. Eickhorst was a lawyer," Teddy said. "Do you happen to know why he is not practicing?"

"I'm afraid you'll have to ask him that, Mr. Roosevelt," Delvecchio said, standing up. "May I wait for your father by the front door?"

"Just through there," Teddy said, inclining his head. "You can wait in the foyer."

Delvecchio nodded.

"Thank you for the breakfast," he said. "I'll see you later, Clint."

Clint nodded and Delvecchio went into the foyer to wait.

"He appears to be loyal," Teddy said. "I wasn't asking him why Mr. Eickhorst doesn't practice, but only if he knew or not."

"I don't think he wants to discuss it at all," Clint said.

"As I said," Teddy repeated, "loyal. That's a good sign."

"And where is my bodyguard?" Theodore, Sr., asked as he came into the dining room again.

"Waiting in the foyer," Teddy replied.

"Well, gentlemen," Theodore said, "let's hope something happens today so we can all go our own ways again, hmm?"

"Stay safe, Father."

"You, too, Teedie."

As the senior Roosevelt went into the foyer—chuckling, Clint thought—Clint looked at Teddy—who was cringing—and repeated, "Teedie?"

"A childhood nickname," Teddy said distastefully. "He did that on purpose."

"Now, now . . . Teedie."

Teddy glared at Clint and said, "Gunsmith!"

And they both cringed.

TWENTY-THREE

At eleven-thirty Clint decided he was going to go
down to Wall Street himself. Teddy had already left to
attend to some business, and to see if he could find out
anything about Sergeant Egan. Clint was simply becoming too impatient to just sit in the Roosevelt house and
wait, or spend his time shooting pool. Besides, the pool
cue had quickly become an extension of his finger, like
his gun, and he rarely—if ever—missed.

He put on the best suit he could find in the closet of
the guest room he was occupying, and as he slipped it
on over his shoulder holster he wished he could just
wear his regular gun belt. In a city like New York,
though, that would simply attract too much attention.

He left the house and headed for Wall Street, after
getting directions from Charles, the houseman, as to
where Theodore Roosevelt's office was.

• • •

"That it?" Haney asked.

"That's the building," Kenrick said. "Roosevelt's got an office in there."

"Ain't his son some kind of big shot politician?" Haney asked.

"Assemblyman," Kenrick replied. "That's not such a big shot."

"Teddy, right? Teddy Roosevelt?"

"What kind of name is that for a grown man?" Kenrick asked. "Teddy."

"How we gonna do this?" Haney asked.

"Well, we aren't going to walk right in there and shoot him," Kenrick said. "We'll wait until he comes out and pick our spot."

"We gonna do this today?"

"That's right."

"No plannin'?"

"According to our employer," Kenrick said, "Roosevelt may know this is coming."

"That's why we need a plan."

"That's why we've got to do this now, without giving him a chance to get ready."

"And what about Adams?"

"He's the man's bodyguard, he should be around."

"How do we know he's his bodyguard?"

"He's staying in the Roosevelt house," Kenrick said, "according to our information. What else would he be doing there?"

"Maybe he's just a guest."

"Well, we'll find out, won't we?" Kenrick said.

"I'd like to find out without comin' face-to-face with the Gunsmith."

"He's just a man."

"That ain't what I heard. I heard he's never missed and never been outdrawn."

"Well," Kenrick said, "there's a first time for everything."

They were in a doorway across from the big brick and concrete building where Theodore Roosevelt, Senior, had his office. Suddenly, Kenrick saw a man walking down the sidewalk toward the building's front door, and he recognized him immediately.

"There he is, there he is," he said, nudging Haney so hard the man yelped in pain.

"What? There who is?"

"Clint Adams."

"Where?"

"Walking toward the front door."

"That's the Gunsmith?"

"That's him."

Haney narrowed his eyes and peered across the street until Clint went into the building.

"He don't look like so much to me."

"You want to switch targets?"

"No, sir," Haney said, "not me. You wanted him, you got him. The Gunsmith is all yours."

"Yes, sir," Kenrick said happily, "he sure is."

TWENTY-FOUR

When Clint got to Theodore Roosevelt's office he found Anson Eickhorst sitting in the waiting room.

"Morning, Adams," Eickhorst said.

"Anson," Clint said. "Where's Mr. Roosevelt?"

"In his office, having a meeting," the man said. "When he's done he said he was going to lunch. What are you doing here?"

Clint sat down next to Eickhorst and smiled disarmingly at the middle-aged woman who was seated at a desk near the door to Roosevelt's office.

"I was getting antsy sitting around the house," Clint said. "Thought I'd come down and take a look at the office, and the area."

"Well, this is it."

"There's a lot of cover outside," Clint said, "lots of windows to fire a gun from."

109

"Don't I know it," Eickhorst said. "It would be easier just to keep Roosevelt in his house and guard him there."

"From what little I know of the man," Clint said, "that would be like trying to cage a hurricane."

"I know what you mean."

They sat in silence for a few moments, the secretary looking up at them from time to time, nervously.

"So, Delvecchio tells me you're a lawyer," Clint finally said.

Eickhorst looked at him for a few seconds, without blinking, before speaking.

"Is this small talk?"

"As a matter of fact," Clint said, "it is. Hey, if you don't want to talk about it—"

"I don't."

"That's fine."

Only the appearance of Theodore Roosevelt, Senior, kept the situation from getting more awkward.

"Mr. Adams," he said in surprise, "what are you doing here?"

"I just wanted to come down and see the layout of the office, and the surrounding areas."

"Well, that's fine," Roosevelt said, handing his secretary some papers. "You know what to do with those, Monica."

"Yes, sir."

Roosevelt looked back at Clint.

"You can join Mr. Eickhorst and myself for lunch."

"Uh, no, I don't think I can do that, sir," Clint said. "I want to take another walk around outside."

"As you wish," Roosevelt said. "Mr. Eickhorst, are you ready?"

"Yes, sir."

Somehow, the respect in Eickhorst's voice surprised Clint, but he supposed Roosevelt inspired that in people.

"We can walk down together, anyway," Roosevelt said.

"Yes, sir," Clint said, "we can do that."

And there it was in his own voice, too.

"Here they come," Haney said.

Across the street Clint, Eickhorst, and Roosevelt were coming out of the building.

"Who's the other man?" Haney asked, squinting.

"Nobody for you to worry about," Kenrick said. "You can handle him."

"You know him?"

"Yeah."

"Who is it?"

"His name's Anson Eickhorst."

"What the hell kind of name is that?"

"I don't know."

"What's he do?"

Kenrick hesitated a moment, then said, "He's a lawyer."

Which, technically, was not a lie.

"They're splittin' up," Haney said.

"Remember," Kenrick said, "you get the banker and I get Adams."

"Sure," Haney said, "I guess I can handle a lawyer, too."

"I guess you can."

TWENTY-FIVE

When the three men split up, Haney took off after the banker and the lawyer, while Kenrick kept pace with Clint Adams, remaining on his side of the street.

He was going to have to pick his spot very carefully.

Clint almost decided to follow along behind Roosevelt and Eickhorst, but they had hired Eickhorst to do a job, and they were going to have to trust him—and Delvecchio—to do it.

In all of Clint's trips to New York he had never been to Wall Street. He was impressed by the buildings, and the conditions of the sidewalk and street, and by the image it presented. It was the banking center of the city, and as such it presented a quiet and dignified front. He had no idea what went on behind the doors and windows, but on the outside everything looked peaceful and quiet.

That was when he heard the shots.

Kenrick had just crossed the street to move in behind Clint Adams when he heard the shots, as well. It shocked him, because he never expected Haney to make his try so soon. He himself had not even had a chance to size Adams up, and suddenly the man was turning and looking at him.

Before he could stop himself, instinct took over and he drew his gun.

Clint turned at the sound of the shot, instinctively knowing that Roosevelt was the target. As he turned he saw a man standing behind him, frozen for a moment, and then the man pulled his gun from inside his jacket.

Clint's hand went into his own jacket, grabbed for the gun in his shoulder holster, and pulled. The hammer caught on the inside fabric of the jacket, almost costing him his life.

The other man had obviously drawn his gun from a shoulder holster before, and he had allowed for the fabric of the jacket. As he pointed his gun at Clint and fired, Clint dropped down into a crouch, yanked his own gun free with a tear, and fired.

The other man's shot missed, going over his head.

Clint's shot did not miss.

Nobody was more surprised than Pete Haney when the lawyer produced a gun and both men fired at the same time.

Haney's hurried shot missed.

Eickhorst's shot did not.

When Clint came around the corner he saw Eickhorst standing over a fallen man. Roosevelt was standing next to him, healthy and safe.

As Clint approached, both men looked at him.

"We heard shots," Roosevelt said.

"Apparently I was a target, as well. Your shots warned me."

"Mr. Eickhorst reacted before I even knew what was going on." Roosevelt was obviously impressed.

"I felt him behind us," Eickhorst said. "I turned, and he drew."

At that point Eickhorst stared curiously at the flap of fabric that was hanging from Clint's jacket.

"Damned shoulder holster," Clint said.

"They take some getting used to."

"Well, I won't have time," Clint said.

"Are you leaving New York?" Roosevelt asked.

"I'd sure like to," Clint said. "I'd like to go back to a place where men wear their guns on the outside, like they're supposed to, but this might just have been a first attempt."

"It's real soon for this to be the only attempt," Eickhorst said.

"I know," Clint said. "Mr. Roosevelt, might I suggest that we go back to your house? Teddy might have some useful information for us."

"We'll have to wait for the police, of course," Roosevelt said.

"Of course," Clint said.

Eickhorst frowned at the mention of the police.

"I'm sure I can hurry things along, however, when they arrive," Roosevelt said. "Did you kill the other man?"

"I did," Clint said.

"Well," Roosevelt said, "both acts were clearly self-defense, and I'll make sure the police know that they were both on my behalf."

"We'd appreciate that, sir," Eickhorst said. "I'd prefer it if I didn't have to spend too much time with them."

"Mr. Eickhorst," Roosevelt said, "because of your actions here today, you are entitled to anything it is in my power to give you."

Eickhorst and Clint exchanged a glance, and then the lawyer looked at the banker.

"I'll be sure to keep that in mind . . . sir," he said.

TWENTY-SIX

It was several hours later when Teddy Roosevelt returned home.

"This is the most amazing thing," he said to all of them—Theodore Senior, Clint, Delvecchio, and Eickhorst.

"What is?" Clint asked.

Teddy knew about the attempt on his father's life, and knew that it had been thwarted.

"The news is all over the street," he said, removing his coat and handing it to the houseman. "Charles, I'll have a glass of sherry."

"Right away, sir."

"Teddy," his father said, "if you don't tell us what you're talking about—"

"I'm talking about the attempt on your life, Father," Teddy said. "It's changed everything."

117

"What's changed?" Clint asked.

"Well," Teddy said, accepting the glass of sherry from Charles, "all morning I could find out nothing about who had put the price on your head, Father. I used every contact I had, and some I didn't have, and there was no information—until this afternoon."

"What happened this afternoon?" Roosevelt, Senior, asked.

"The attempt on your life, sir," Eickhorst said.

"Or rather," Delvecchio added, "the failure of it."

"That's it precisely," Teddy said. "Everyone is so impressed with how quickly the attempt was put down that no one else wants to try."

"That's amazing," Theodore said.

"So we're out of jobs," Delvecchio said.

"Not at all," Theodore said. "You fellows are employed for as long as you like, at double the salary—that goes for you, too, Mr. Adams."

"Not me," Clint said. "If the immediate danger is over, I'm getting on a train and heading back west."

"Without giving me a chance to get even at pool?" Teddy asked.

"Another time, Teddy," Clint promised. "Another time."

"What about the lady?" Teddy asked.

Clint smiled.

"One last night to say good-bye," Clint said, "and then I'm on a train."

Theodore got up from his seat and approached Clint with his hand out.

"I can't tell you how much I appreciate what you've done," he said.

"It was my pleasure, sir," he said. "I think you'll be safe with these two fellas on the job."

"I'm keeping them on to keep my entire family safe," Roosevelt, Sr., said.

"I think they'll do the job."

With that Clint went upstairs to pack his things, thankful that this job had not dragged on and kept him in New York any longer. He longed for the open space of the West, and he missed Duke, his big black gelding.

Time to go.

PART TWO
Little Missouri
Five months later . . .

TWENTY-SEVEN

Little Missouri, in the Dakota Territory, wasn't much. Clint could see that as he stepped off the Northern Pacific. A few ramshackle buildings unevenly spaced, dwarfed by buttes on both sides.

Clint walked back to the livestock car to claim Duke. He and his horse were the only ones getting off at this stop.

Once Clint and Duke were clear, the train started up again and continued west, to the end of the line. In point of fact the Northern Pacific had only recently completed laying track, and the railroad construction gangs—not to mention the military that were assigned to protect them— had only recently pulled out. Little Missouri, or "Little Misery," as the fifty or sixty residents of the town called it, was not wide open to white man and Indian alike, and only time would tell what the outcome would be.

Clint didn't know a lot of this as he watched the train pull away. All he knew was that he had been invited by a friend, Bill Merrifield, who had started the Maltese Cross Ranch with his friend, Sylvane Ferris. Both men were Canadians, which was all Clint knew of what they had in common.

Clint waited about fifteen minutes and when Merrifield did not arrive he mounted Duke and rode him into town. The largest of the shacks were the Pyramid Park Hotel and a nearby saloon called Big-Mouthed Bob's Bug Juice Dispensary. The saloon advertised in its window that it served something called "Forty-Mile Red." There were also three or four buildings on the opposite side of the tracks.

Having expected to be met by his friend Merrifield, Clint decided to wait in the saloon. He left Duke outside, loosely tying him to the hitching post. Duke wouldn't have gone anywhere even left untied, but Clint didn't want to invite anyone to try and make off with the gelding. He didn't want to end up having to pay some poor bastard's doctor bills. Duke might have been getting old, but he still had all his teeth, and he knew how to use them.

Clint found the saloon empty except for the bartender, who was wiping at the bar listlessly with a dirty rag. As Clint entered, the man looked up and stopped wiping. He smiled, revealing more spaces than teeth. He wondered if this was Bob, and if the loss of teeth was a result of drinking his own bug juice.

"Afternoon, mister," the bartender said.

"Afternoon."

"What kin I getcha?" the man asked. "Some Forty-mile Red-eye, maybe?"

"Uh, no," Clint said. "You wouldn't be, uh, Bob, would you?"

"That's me," the man said, "Big-Mouthed Bob they call me. Know why?"

"Uh, no, I don't."

"It's 'cause I got so many teeth—well, I had so many teeth when I was younger. Truth of it is I been losin' them some, lately."

"Is that a fact?"

"Yeah, see?" Bob smiled to illustrate his point.

"Uh, yeah, I see," Clint said. "Had to have them pulled?"

"Hell no," Bob said, "they's jest fallin' out for some reason."

"Do you drink your own liquor?"

"Sure do," Bob said. "I wouldn't serve the public somethin' I don't drink myself."

He had no idea that Clint's question had to do with his losing his teeth. He thought they'd gone on to another subject entirely.

"Have you got any beer?"

"Sure do," Bob said. "An' it's cold, too."

"I'll have a beer."

"Comin' right up."

He came back with a frosty mug of beer, which Clint fervently hoped was as good as it looked. Much to his surprise—and delight—it was.

"Sure is nice ta see somebody in here in the middle of the day," Bob said.

"I just got off the train."

"A purpose?"

Clint could well understand the question.

"Yes, on purpose," he said. "I was supposed to be met by my friend, Bill Merrifield."

"You a friend of Bill's?"

"Yes, I am. Do you know him?"

"Sure do."

"Have you seen him around today?"

"Sure ain't."

Clint drained his beer, slaking his thirst, and asked, "Can I have another?"

"Sure can."

Bob returned with a second beer and said, "This one's on the house."

"Well, thanks, Bob."

"I jest glad to have some company. You goin' inta business with ol' Bill and his partner?"

"Sylvane Ferris, you mean?"

"That's him."

"Why would you think I was going into partnership with them?"

"Everybody knows they's in trouble and are lookin' for a partner to bail 'em out."

"Bail them out," Clint asked, "or buy them out?"

"Them boys don't want to sell," Bob said. "They jest need some help."

Clint wondered if that was why Merrifield had invited him. If it was, his friend was in for a disappointment. Clint didn't have the money to invest in a failing ranch.

"You best wait here for Merrifield," Bob said. "If he's supposed to meet you, he'll look here first."

"What's the Pyramid Park Hotel like?"

"You don't want to stay there," Bob said. "They rent cots, not rooms. Like as not you'd have to share a room with thirteen or fourteen other men."

"What kind of a hotel is that?"

Bob shrugged.

"That's the Pyramid Park," he said. "It's run by the Captain."

"Why's he called the Captain?"

"That's from his steamboat days," Bob said. "Foulest mouth on the Missouri, that was the Captain, and his mouth ain't got any better since he's been on dry land."

"I guess I'll wait for Merrifield, then," Clint said. "Mind if I take my beer to a table?"

"Help yourself," Bob said. "Jest give me a wave when you're ready for another one."

"I think I'll nurse this one for a while," Clint said, picking the fresh one up from the bar.

"Like as not it'll get warm," Bob said. "When you get halfway I'll bring a fresh one. No extra charge."

"I appreciate that, Bob."

Clint took the beer and picked a table all the way in the back, where he sat with his back to the wall to wait for Bill Merrifield.

TWENTY-EIGHT

Bob kept replenishing Clint's beer each time it got to the halfway mark and had done that twice more before another customer entered the saloon, and three times before Bill Merrifield walked through the front doors.

"What took you so long?" Clint asked as Merrifield approached his table.

"I got stuck out at the ranch," Merrifield said. "When did you get in?"

"On time."

Clint stood and the two men shook hands. Merrifield was in his thirties, a pleasant-looking man with an easygoing manner.

"Sorry you had to wait, Clint," he said. "Did Bob treat you okay?"

"Keeps bringing me fresh beers," Clint said, "no charge."

"You didn't drink none of that Forty-Mile, did you?" Merrifield asked.

"Not after the first time Bob smiled at me."

"Good," Merrifield said. "That stuff'll rot your innards *and* your teeth. Come on, I'll take you out to the ranch."

On the way out Clint stopped at the bar to thank Big-Mouthed Bob for looking out for him.

"Glad for the company," Bob said. "Come on back in when you're in town."

"I will."

They passed two more men coming in as they left, which gave Bob three customers.

"This a full house for him?" Clint asked.

"There's only fifty or sixty people living in Little Misery," Merrifield said. "Sooner or later they all come to Bob's."

"Little Misery?"

"That's what the folks hereabouts call it."

"I thought there'd be a lot more people than this," Clint said outside. "What happened?"

"Railroad finished laying track," Merrifield said. "Their crews left, and so did the soldiers who were protecting them. We're on our own now."

There was a bay standing next to Duke, and Merrifield walked to it and mounted up.

"Come on," he said, "we'll talk on the way to the ranch."

During the ride Merrifield explained Little Misery's plight. With the railroad gone the town was up for grabs.

"In fact, yesterday sort of signified the changes around here."

"What happened yesterday?"

"The Golden Spike Special passed through, on its way to the end of the line in Montana. Grant himself was on board."

Clint had met the former president while Grant was still in office, but did not mention this.

"So what do you plan to do?" he asked.

"Me and Ferris are gonna hold on to our ranch," Merrifield said.

"I heard you've had some trouble and are looking for a partner."

"Not you," Merrifield said. "I know you're not a rancher, Clint. We got somebody in mind, though."

"Oh, who's that?"

"This dandy came to town a couple of weeks ago, all the way from New York. He wanted to go buffalo hunting."

"Are there any left?"

"Not many," Merrifield said. "He hired my partner's brother, Joe, to guide him. If anyone can find some buffalo left around here, Joe Ferris can."

"What makes you think he'll want to be partners?"

"He likes the West, and he likes this area. Also, Sylvane asked Joe to work on him while they were out. They should be back sometime tomorrow, or the next day."

"Does this New York dandy have a name?" Clint asked.

"Sure he does," Merrifield said. "It's, uh, now what the hell is it? Oh, yeah, I think he said his name was Roosevelt."

TWENTY-NINE

"He's got that much money?" Merrifield asked.

"If it's the same Roosevelt," Clint said, "and I can't imagine that there'd be another one like him."

They were approaching the ranch, which wasn't much to look at as ranches go. Merrifield and Ferris had built the house themselves, and neither man particularly claimed to be a great house builder. The logs were straight, though, and the roof was still on. The windows were a little crooked, but there was no glass in them, so it really didn't matter much—except in the winter.

"I know it doesn't look like much," Merrifield said, "but some fresh money would help a lot."

"Roosevelt money," Clint said.

"Hey," Merrifield said, "if he wants to buy in, who are we to say no?"

"Bill—"

"Come on," Merrifield said, cutting him off before he could protest, "I'll introduce you to my partner."

They dismounted in front of the house.

"We can take care of the horses later," Merrifield said. "Come inside."

They walked into the house and Clint saw a man in his mid-thirties trying to mend a hole in his pants with a needle and thread.

"Sylvane, this is my friend, Clint Adams," Merrifield said. "Clint, Sylvane Ferris, my partner."

Ferris stood up and shook hands with Clint, shifting the needle to his left hand to do it.

"Glad to meet you," he said. "Bill's told me a lot about you."

"Wait until you hear what Clint told me about this Roosevelt fella who's hunting with Joe."

"What about him?"

"He's rich."

"We knew that."

"No," Merrifield said, "we thought that, but he never came right out and said it."

"He offered my brother a lot of money to take him buffalo hunting."

"I know," Merrifield said, "but now we know for *sure* that he's rich."

"Is he a friend of yours?" Sylvane asked Clint.

"Yes, he is."

Sylvane looked at his partner.

"Bill, maybe we better rethink this."

"Why?"

"Well, if he's a friend of Clint's, maybe we shouldn't be trying to convince him to buy in."

"Yeah," Merrifield said, "but what if he wants to buy in?"

"Well, that'd be different," Sylvane said. He looked at Clint. "Does your friend want to be a rancher?"

"I don't honestly know, Sylvane," Clint said. "I guess you'd have to ask him."

Sylvane looked at his partner.

"If he's that rich there's lots of other places he could invest in a ranch than here in the Badlands."

"But he's here," Merrifield said. "Why don't we just wait for the man to come back and speak for himself, huh?"

Sylvane looked at Clint.

"It makes sense to me," Clint said with a shrug.

"Are you gonna be staying with us?" Sylvane asked. "We've got room."

"We can't let him stay at the Pyramid Park," Merrifield said. "Of course he's staying with us."

"Where's your horse?"

"Out front," Clint said.

"With mine," Merrifield said.

Sylvane put down his needle and thread and his trousers and said, "I'll see to them." He looked at Clint. "I'll bring in your saddlebags."

"Thanks."

"Why don't you get him settled, and give him a cup of coffee?" Sylvane said.

"Sure," Merrifield said, "then we can show him around the place."

Sylvane stopped at the door.

"You're not gonna try to get him to invest, too, are you?"

"No, no," Merrifield said, "I just want to show him what we've got."

"Because too many partners . . . that's trouble, you know?" Sylvane said to both of them.

"You don't have to worry," Clint said. "I'm just passing through."

Sylvane nodded and left the house.

"Your partner seems to have more scruples than you do," Clint said.

"Those ain't scruples," Merrifield said. "He just doesn't like people much, so he's never had a partner before me."

"Maybe you shouldn't take on another one, then. Did you ever think of that?"

"We need the money, Clint," Merrifield said. "That's all this place needs is some money to get it started. Hey, maybe your friend would like to be a silent and absent partner?"

"Again," Clint said, "you're going to have to ask him, Bill."

"What's he do back there in New York that makes him so rich?"

"His father's a banker and a rich man," Clint said, "and Teddy's a politician."

"Teddy?"

"Didn't you know his first name?"

"Not really."

"It's Theodore," Clint said. "His name is Theodore Roosevelt, Jr., and when I was in New York five months ago I helped to save his father's life."

"Well, then," Merrifield said, "I guess that makes him beholden to you, huh?"

"Forget it, Bill," Clint said. "You can make your own pitch."

"Okay, okay," Merrifield said, "you're right. I'm not gonna ask you to get involved."

"Good," Clint said. "Now how about that coffee?"

THIRTY

After dinner—prepared by Sylvane, who seemed to be the cook of the two partners—they took Clint out and showed him their ranch. Right now it was a few horses and a hundred and fifty head of cattle on good grazing land, and lots of that.

"How did you manage that?" Clint asked

"Well," Merrifield said, somewhat sheepishly, "they're not really ours. See, we bought them with money we got from a couple of fellas who live in Minnesota and we run them for them. We get a portion of the profits."

"So you've already got absentee partners," Clint said.

"Not in the ranch," Merrifield said, "just in the cattle."

It sounded to Clint like six of one and half a dozen of another, but he didn't say anything.

He rode with the two partners over most of their lands and had to admit that they had a nice spread.

"We know we do," Merrifield said, "now we just have to be able to keep it."

"Is there somebody trying to take it away from you?" Clint asked.

"Somebody is always trying to take what's yours," Sylvane said.

"Never mind that," Merrifield said. "Clint doesn't have to get involved in that."

It sounded to Clint like he was being set up to ask what "that" was, so he didn't. If Merrifield had something he wanted to talk about, Clint's attitude was let him bring it up himself.

Later they all decided to go into town.

"Big-Mouthed Bob's is the only place to find any action," Merrifield said, "but you're likely to find a poker game, or a woman, that might strike your fancy— especially now."

"Why now?" Clint asked.

"The soldiers are gone," Sylvane said.

"And the railroad workers," Merrifield said. "See, they were the ones with the money."

Clint wondered what kind of women a town like this would offer.

"Sounds like the competition for the women left, but so did the poker players."

"No," Sylvane said. "The railroad workers played only among themselves."

"And the soldiers?"

"They had enough money for women, or poker, but not both," Merrifield said.

"Are the women at Big-Mouthed Bob's worth passing up a poker game?"

Sylvane and Merrifield exchanged a glance, and Merrifield said, "I think we'll let you judge that for yourself."

During the trip to town Merrifield and Sylvane Ferris told Clint about the "crazy Frenchman" who had come to the area.

"His name's—what's his name, Sylvane?"

"Antoine-Amedee-Marie-Vincent-Amat Manca de Valombrosa, Marquis de Mores."

Merrifield shook his head and chuckled.

"I don't know how he remembers all that," he said to Clint.

"How could you forget a name like that?" Sylvane asked.

Clint tended to side with Merrifield.

"I'll just think of him as the Marquis de Mores," he decided. "What makes him crazy?"

"Well, for one thing," Merrifield said, "he set up camp on the other side of the river, and then decided he'd start his own town. He's calling it—what's he calling it?" Merrifield asked Sylvane.

"Medora," Sylvane said, "after his wife."

"I see. Why is he here?"

Merrifield looked at Sylvane, who seemed to have the better memory of the two men.

"He intends to use Badlands beef to buy himself the crown of France."

Clint frowned.

"Why do I suspect there's more to it than that?" he asked.

"You'll meet him, I'm sure," Sylvane said. "He'll tell you the full story."

"Anyway," Merrifield said, "nobody around here wants to have anything to do with the crazy little son of a bitch."

"Except Paddock," Sylvane reminded him.

"Who?" Clint asked.

"E. G. Paddock," Merrifield said. "Biggest man in these parts, and he seems to want to ally himself with that Frenchman—God only knows why."

"Maybe he wants to be a prince of France, or something," Clint said.

"Who knows?" Merrifield said. "I think they're both crazy."

"Like a couple of foxes," Sylvane said.

"Sylvane doesn't think the Marquis' plan is so far-fetched."

"I don't think he can buy himself the crown of France," Sylvane said, "but I think his plans might make him a ton of money."

"Sylvane also thinks we could make some money, too," Merrifield said, "but first we need money to invest."

"It takes money to make money."

Clint certainly agreed with that, whether you were talking about ranching or gambling.

THIRTY-ONE

They reached town and left their horses in front of the saloon. There were no other horses there, but when they walked inside it was clear to Clint that most of the men in town were in the saloon.

"Remember," Merrifield said, "stay away from the Forty-Mile Red-eye."

"I'll stick with beer," Clint said.

Bob waved them over with a big smile, and the three of them walked to the bar and ordered beer.

"Didn't expect you back so soon," he said to Clint.

"What else is there to do around here, Bob?" Merrifield asked.

"And I want to keep it that way," Bob shot back.

Clint turned his back to the bar and checked out the room. There were three poker games going on, and eight or nine more tables of men sitting and talking. Working the room were three girls and, to Clint's surprise, they were all young and beautiful.

"You noticed the girls, huh?" Bob asked.

"Now, don't take offense at this, Bob," Clint said, "but how did you convince those three lovelies to come here to Little Missouri?"

"I convinced them that there was money to be made here in Little Misery," Bob said.

"Well, while the railroad was here that was true," Merrifield said. "How are you gonna keep 'em here now that the railroad and the soldiers are gone?"

"I'll just have to convince them that Little Misery's gonna grow," Bob said.

"And how do you think that's gonna happen?"

"Maybe that Frenchie'll have something to do with it."

"Him," Merrifield said. "He started his own town, remember? Maybe he'll come over here and steal your girls."

"He better not try," Bob said, "no, sir." Big-Mouthed Bob gritted what teeth he had left when he said that. Clint thought it was a frightful sight.

"I see an opening at one of the poker games," Merrifield said. "You want to take it, Clint?"

"No, you go ahead," Clint said. "I just want to watch the action for a while."

Merrifield took his beer and hurried over to take the open chair.

"Tell me something, Sylvane?" Clint asked.

"What's that?"

"You and Bill don't seem to see eye to eye on a lot of things."

"Sure we do," Sylvane said. "It's just that I remember what we agree on, and he doesn't."

"Bill told me it's your brother who took Roosevelt out buffalo hunting."

"Talk about crazy Frenchmen," Sylvane said, "there's one crazy dude from New York."

"No buffalo left, huh?"

"In the past four months about fifteen thousand buffalo have been slaughtered, believe it or not."

Clint whistled.

"By who?"

"Sioux, mostly. Some of them were shot by white men traveling through on the train."

"What do the federals think of that?"

"They encouraged the Sioux," Sylvane said. "They figure as soon as all the buffalo are gone, the Sioux will be gone, too."

"I think they have a point. Will your brother be able to find any buffalo for Roosevelt to hunt?"

"Who knows?" Sylvane said.

They were interrupted when one of the girls came up to them to talk to Sylvane, who smiled widely and put his arm around her.

"Clint, this is Rose, Bob's best girl."

"Huh," Rose said, "you tell us all that."

"You're all his best girls, then."

Rose was about twenty-five, short and buxom, dark-haired and pale-skinned. She had a very pretty face with just the hint of a double chin.

"Are you ready for me?" Sylvane asked her.

"I just happen to have an opening," she said, and then giggled.

"See you later, Clint," Sylvane said.

"Maybe your friend wants to come along?" she asked. "He's very good-looking."

"I'll bet you say that to all the men," Clint said.

"I'll bet I don't," she said. "Look at this one. Ugly as sin."

"But I make up for it in other ways," Sylvane said, and the two went off, arms around each other. It was the most animated Clint had seen Sylvane Ferris since meeting him.

THIRTY-TWO

Upstairs Sylvane watched Rose undress and smiled as her plump but firm breasts came into view. When she was naked she came to him on the bed and pulled down his trousers. He'd been with her enough times that she knew what he liked. She licked her lips as his erection came into view, then cradled it in her hands and lowered her head. She licked the shaft, then a place just below the head, and then the head itself. Finally, she engulfed him completely in her mouth, and he groaned and reached for her. He put one hand on her head and slid the other beneath her to cup one of her breasts, squeezing the nipple at the same time. She moaned with her mouth full, a sound that inflamed him even more. To him there could be nothing better than this, than having a whore take him in her mouth and suck him.

Unless it was getting that Roosevelt fella to invest some money in the Maltese Cross Ranch.

Clint spent the next couple of hours watching the poker games from the bar. He was able to tell who was winning and who was losing from there. It looked to him like Merrifield had started out losing and simply continued from there.

He also spent time looking at the women. Big-Mouthed Bob seemed to have himself a nice little selection: the little brunette who had gone upstairs with Sylvane—and still had not come down, by the way—a slender blonde with a small but full-lipped mouth and a lean, small-breasted body. The third girl was a redhead who seemed to be the oldest of the three, almost thirty, and she wore the extra years like extra experience. She walked differently than the other two. Rather than a saucy swish of her hips and butt, she moved across the room as if she were gliding, her chin held high so that her long, graceful neck was shown off to its best advantage. She was neither buxom nor small-breasted and seemed a happy medium between the other two women. If Clint was in the habit of paying for sex—and he wasn't—he would have chosen her. He preferred experience over youth every time.

Finally, after two full hours, Sylvane came downstairs with the dark-haired girl, and she began to once again circulate through the room.

Clint had seen the blonde go upstairs and come back down again with three different men during the time Sylvane had been upstairs with Rose.

From Bob he found out that the blonde's name was Esther, while the redhead's name was Dulcy.

When Sylvane came down there was an empty chair at one of the other poker games, and he took it. When a chair opened at the third table, Clint moved into it. Since he was the guest of both Merrifield and Sylvane, he did not want to play against them.

"The game's dealer's choice, friend," one of the men said. "Two-dollar limit, up to five dollars on the last round."

Clint had played in smaller games. In fact, he knew that the game Merrifield was in was for quarters. He'd play poker for a nickel or five dollars, mostly for the pure enjoyment of the game. He'd also been in games where there was thousands of dollars on the table.

A famous gambler had once told him, "We don't play for money, that's just our way of keeping score," and it had always stuck with him.

"Are you in?" the dealer asked him, tossing in his own ante.

Clint tossed a dollar into the pot and said, "I'm in."

After an hour Clint was comfortably ahead. There were four other players at the table, and only one of them was also ahead. Of the other three, two of them were getting grumpy about losing—or about Clint's winning.

"You ain't lost a pot since you sat down, stranger," one of them said.

Clint looked at him. He didn't remember the man's name. In fact, if he'd heard their names at all during the game he had forgotten them.

"Sure I have, friend," Clint said. "You've just got to keep your eye on the game."

"Well," the man said, "you ain't lost many. I seen that, sure enough."

"Well, you're probably right about that," Clint said. "The cards do seem to be coming my way."

As he said that the dealer tossed him an ace of spades. He checked his hole cards and found the ace of hearts and the ace of diamonds.

"Bet the ace," the dealer said.

THIRTY-THREE

"A dollar," Clint said, not wanting to force anyone out too soon.

The man who had been complaining seemed to suddenly have become happy. He had a king of diamonds in front of him.

"Raise two dollars," he said.

He was proud of something, and it had to be more than just one king.

The other three players stayed in, although none had a face card on the table. Clint had noticed after the first five hands he played that most of the players at the table didn't like to go out before the last card. It was as if they expected some miracle to suddenly improve the other six cards by the time the seventh came along.

The other player who was ahead had a nine of clubs on the table. He was also the dealer.

"Comin' out," he said and dealt out the fourth card.

For Clint it was a useless three of spades, but the man with the king on the table got another one, this one a king of hearts.

"Check to the raiser," Clint said.

The man frowned, because he *had* wanted to raise again now that he had another king. If he'd raised before because he had three of them, Clint thought, he now had an almost unbeatable hand of four kings. However, since the man had been losing steadily, Clint felt he might have raised before on the strength of two kings, which would give him three at the moment.

Everyone called the bet, including Clint.

"Fifth card," the dealer said and dealt Clint a three of hearts. He now had a full house, aces over threes.

The man with the pair of kings on the table got a ten of hearts, which didn't help much.

"Two dollars," he said, tossing his money in the pot.

Everyone stayed, and then Clint said, "Raise two."

"Ha!" said the man with the kings. "Pair of threes. You're bluffing. I raise two dollars."

One player finally folded, but the others stayed, and Clint called.

"Sixth card comin'," the dealer said and doled them out. He got a pair of nines. Clint didn't improve, drawing a two of hearts.

The man with the kings got another ten, and now had a full house, kings over tens.

The fourth king in the deck had fallen across the table from Clint, so he knew the best hand the man could have was a full house—which he had beat.

"Two pair bets," the dealer said.

"Ya can't make any money this way," the man said.

"How about we bet five dollars on this round?"

The dealer shrugged and said, "That's up to everyone else."

"I'm out," one of the men said, "so I got no say."

"I'm gonna fold anyway," the man across from Clint said, "so I don't, either."

The dealer had his pair of nines on the table and said, "It's fine with me. What about you?" he asked Clint.

"Somebody's going to be disappointed," Clint said warningly.

"Ha!" the man with the kings and tens said. "Yeah, you! Whataya, scared?"

"Fine, then," Clint said. "Raise the bet."

"Five dollars on two pair," the bettor said.

The dealer stayed in with his nines. Clint was starting to wonder what he had.

"I call," he said, "and raise five dollars."

"Bluffing," the two pair said. "I raise another five dollars."

"Okay," said the dealer, "I'll raise, too."

"What?" the man with two pair said. "With nines?"

"How many of those do you have?" Clint asked.

The man smiled and said, "At least two."

"Hmmm," Clint said. "I call."

"Call," the original bettor said. Clint could see he was starting to sweat. He had kings full, and he was starting to think he wasn't going to win.

"Last card," the dealer said and dealt them out to the three remaining players. Clint lifted one edge of the card so he could take a quick look.

"Two pair bets," the dealer said.

The man studied Clint and the dealer. If he thought

Clint was bluffing, what were the chances the dealer was also bluffing?

"Ten dollars!" he said forcefully. "If we went to five on the last round, we can go ten on this one."

"Fine," the dealer said, not bothering to check with Clint. "I raise ten."

"And so do I," Clint said.

"Wha—who—how—" the man with two pair stammered. "You're both bluffin'!"

"Only one way to find out, friend," the dealer said.

"I ain't foldin'!" he cried out.

"Which is probably your problem," Clint said, "the whole game."

"Oh yeah?" the man said. "Well . . . I bet twenty."

"You raise twenty?" the dealer asked.

"Yeah, yeah, that's what I mean."

"Your twenty," the dealer said, "and twenty more."

"I'll have to do that, too," Clint said.

The dealer looked across the table at the man with two pair—and probably kings full—and said, "Forty to you."

"I—I ain't got forty dollars left."

"You should have thought of that before you started raising the stakes," the dealer said. "Either call the deal or fold."

"You—you're tryin' to steal it."

"You poor bastard," one of the other men at the table said, "they ain't both bluffing. One of them's got to have you beat."

"Not with what I got," the man complained.

"Everybody at the table knows you got kings full, Zack."

"Whataya tellin' my hand—"

"He's right, Zack," the dealer said. "You're beat."

"With a full house?"

"Call the bet," the dealer said, "or fold."

"Loan me some money!" the man said to the other players, but they refused.

He looked around.

"Somebody loan me forty dollars."

No one stepped forward.

"You're out," the dealer said. "I'll call—"

"Hey, wait—"

"You're out, friend," the dealer said, tossing twenty dollars into the pot. "What do you have?" he asked Clint.

Clint turned over his hole cards, revealing three aces.

"Four aces," one of the other players breathed.

"Son of a bitch," the dealer said and turned over his hole cards to show that he had four nines.

"Two hands of four of a kind," somebody said.

"I had kings—kings full," Zack complained.

"You're lucky you didn't have more money, Zack," one of the other players said. "You would have lost it all."

"Nice hand, friend," the dealer said to Clint.

"That's the best hand I ever had," Zack said in disbelief. "Th-there can't be two four of a kinds in one hand. There can't!"

"Forget it, Zack," the man next to him said. "Go on home. Marie's waiting for you."

"They cheated," Zack said, shaking his head. His eyes looked blank, as if he was incapable of hearing anything anyone was saying. "They cheated."

"Both of them?" his friend asked. The man reached

out and grabbed Zack's arm to shake him. "Go home. Don't make it worse."

Zack shook off his hands and continued to stare down at his cards.

"I need the cards," Clint said. He was the next dealer.

Zack didn't move, so the man next to him pushed the cards over to Clint. It was the sudden absence of the cards that seemed to shake Zack from his reverie. He looked around the table, then pushed his chair back slowly and stood up. Clint watched him carefully, because the man was wearing a gun. In fact, everybody at the table was watching him, and so were some of the others in the saloon.

He stood there for a few moments, then slowly, listlessly made his way to the front door and went out.

The tension in the air broke with an almost audible snap.

THIRTY-FOUR

"Jesus," the fourth man at the table said. "I thought he was gonna do something stupid."

"He still might," said Zack's friend. "I'd be careful if I was you two."

"Is there a lawman in town?" the man who had the four nines asked.

This was the first inkling Clint had that this man was also a stranger in town.

"Nearest sheriff is a hundred and fifty miles to the east, and the closest marshal is two hundred miles south," Zack's friend said.

"What's your name?" Clint asked him.

"Me? Len Varney."

"Is Zack a friend of yours, Len?"

"I guess."

"Is he likely to try something tonight?"

"I don't rightly know," Varney said. "Maybe."

"What about that town across the river?"

"Ain't hardly a town yet," Varney said. "There's some buildings there, and that crazy Frenchman's almost got his slaughterhouse ready."

"Slaughterhouse?" the other stranger asked.

Varney nodded.

"He's got it in his mind to slaughter his beef here himself and then ship it that way," Varney said. "Says he's gonna make a ton of money that way."

"I saw the chimney earlier today," the stranger said. "There's also a house on a hill that looks kind of grand."

"That's the Marquis' house," Varney said. "He can look down on Little Misery and his town from there, once it's done. He's gonna be the Lord of the Manor, he thinks."

"Are we playing cards?" the other man at the table asked.

"We need a fifth," Varney said, looking around. "Gotta have five for a decent game."

No sooner had he said that than a man detached himself from the bar and walked over.

"Mind if I sit in?" he asked.

"New hand just startin'," Varney said and explained the rules to the man.

The game went on for about another hour and by the end Clint was well ahead. The other stranger had just about broken even, and the other three men were the losers. The fifth man, who had only sat in an hour ago, had lost only a few dollars.

"I've had enough," Varney said.

"Me, too," said the man across from Clint.

The stranger looked around the room.

"Looks like there's some room at one of the other tables."

"Smaller game over there," Varney said.

"A game's a game," the man said. "Anyone else interested in the chair?"

"Not me," the fifth man said.

"You take it," Clint said, "I'm going to get a beer."

"Don't drink while you play, eh?" the stranger asked.

"I like to be able to see my cards," Clint said.

"You see 'em real well, mister," the man said. "You play real well." He stood up. "It was a pleasure watching you work."

He extended his hand and Clint shook it.

"It's not work to me," Clint said.

"Seems to me it could be," the man said, and wandered over to the table Sylvane Ferris was sitting at.

Clint stood up, turned toward the bar, and saw Bill Merrifield standing there with a beer. His game was still going on, but he had quit it a while back.

Clint joined him at the bar and ordered a beer.

"Looks like you did all right."

"I won a few dollars," Clint said, picking up his beer. "You know a fella named Zack?"

"Zack? Sure, what about him?"

"He lost a lot of money," Clint said, "lost with kings full."

Merrifield whistled.

"Who beat him?"

"Four nines and four aces," Clint said. "I had the aces."

"His wife's gonna kill him if he lost all his money," Merrifield said.

"Yeah, a friend of his said something about his wife," Clint said. "Marie's her name?"

Merrifield nodded.

"I don't know what a woman like Marie is doin' with Zack," Merrifield said.

"Is she too good for him, then?"

"She is," Merrifield said, "and she's a beauty, too. "It's hard to figure what draws some women to some men."

"I guess so. He took losing hard, especially that last hand. Is he liable to try to get the money back?"

"How do you mean?"

"I mean without waiting for another game."

"Oh," Merrifield said, "you know, I don't rightly know about that."

"I understand the law's pretty far away."

"You got that right. If he does try anything, you'll have every right to defend yourself."

"You know a Len Varney?"

"Sure, I know Len."

"I figure he's a friend of Zack's. Maybe he can talk to him."

"I wouldn't rightly call them friends," Merrifield said.

"What would you call them?"

"Me?" Merrifield asked. "Well, I'm old-fashioned. I'd call them brothers. Zack's last name is Varney."

THIRTY-FIVE

"I don't get it," Clint said.

"What don't you get?" Merrifield asked.

They had been joined by Sylvane, who had left his poker game.

"That fella you sent over started winnin' all the money," he'd complained.

"I didn't send him over," Clint had said, but Sylvane continued to brood into his beer.

"I don't get how two men can be brothers and not be friends," Clint continued now.

That drew Sylvane's attention.

"You got a brother?" he asked.

"No."

"That explains it, then."

"Explains what?"

"Explains why you can't understand it."

"Aren't you and your brother friends?"

"Well, sure," Sylvane said, "but we like each other."

"All brothers don't like each other?"

"Did the Earps like each other?" Sylvane asked. He knew that Clint was friends with the Earp family.

"Well . . . yeah, they did."

"All the time?" Sylvane asked. "They never argued?"

"Well, sure they argued," Clint said. "They're human, after all."

"There you go," Sylvane said. "You answered your own question."

"I guess I did," Clint agreed.

"Time to go," Merrifield said.

"Home?" Clint asked.

"Naw," Merrifield said, "I got to go upstairs."

"With Rose?"

"No," Merrifield said, "Esther. I like my woman tall and lean."

"I like them small and plump," Sylvane said.

"How about you, Clint?"

"Smart," Clint said. "I like them smart."

Both men frowned.

"You wouldn't sleep with a dumb woman?" Merrifield asked.

"Sure, I would," Clint said, "but she wouldn't be my first choice."

"What if the dumb one was better looking than the smart one?" Sylvane asked.

"Are they both pretty?"

"Sure," Sylvane said, "neither one is ugly, but the dumb one is better looking than the smart one."

"I guess I'd pick the smart one, then," Clint said.

"Give me the good-lookin' one every time," Merrifield said. "See you boys later."

"What time does Big-Mouthed Bob's stay open until?" Clint asked Sylvane.

"As long as somebody's here," Sylvane said, "he stays open."

"Well," Clint said, "if you don't mind I'm going to go back to the ranch and get some sleep."

"I'll come with you," Sylvane said. "I'll just tell Bob to tell Bill we left."

"I'll meet you outside," Clint said.

"Right."

Clint went to the door while Sylvane moved down the bar to talk to Bill. As Clint stepped out he felt something in the wind, and Duke suddenly kicked up a fuss. It was the only explanation for why he suddenly dropped down as a shot rang out and a bullet whizzed over his head. Once again his inexplicable sixth sense—and Duke— had saved his life.

Upstairs Bill Merrifield had Esther's hips in his hands and he was looking down at her taut bare butt. He was about to slide his penis between her thighs and enter her from behind when he heard the shot.

"No, no, no," he said, shaking his head and stroking one bare butt cheek.

"Bill?"

She reached behind and took hold of his erect penis and pulled on it gently.

"Ah, the hell with it," he said, and slid into her from behind.

•   •   •

"What the hell—" Sylvane shouted. He came running out the door with his gun drawn.

"Get down!" Clint shouted.

Sylvane dropped down next to Clint, who also had his gun out.

"Who is it?" he asked.

"I don't know," Clint said. "I didn't see anyone."

They waited a few moments, but there were no further shots. No one else came out of the saloon. If Bill Merrifield had heard the shot, he wasn't letting it interfere with what he was doing.

Clint stood up slowly, followed by Sylvane.

"He's gone," Clint said.

"Where was he?"

"I don't know that, either."

"How did you manage to avoid getting shot?" Sylvane asked.

"Just lucky, I guess," Clint said. "I just sort of felt there was someone out there, and I ducked just in time."

"That's not luck," Sylvane said, holstering his gun, "that's goddamned spooky."

"Maybe," Clint said, holstering his own weapon. "I want to take a look across the street."

They both crossed over and looked around the storefronts, but there were no telltale signs that the gunman had been there.

"What about the roof?" Sylvane asked.

"No, it didn't come from above."

"Then maybe it came from inside one of the stores."

"Yeah," Clint said, "but which one?"

"The general store might be interesting."

"Why's that?" Clint asked.

"Because it's owned by Len and Zack Varney."

"That is interesting," Clint said. "I guess I should pay the Varneys a visit tomorrow, just to have a talk."

"Maybe I'll come along," Sylvane said, "if you don't mind."

"I don't mind at all," Clint said.

THIRTY-SIX

When they said they had plenty of room for Clint to sleep, they didn't mention that they didn't have a bed.

"Just throw a blanket down anywhere," Sylvane said, on his way to his own bed. "Just don't block the door or Bill will trip over you when he comes back."

Clint pitched his blanket on the floor of the main room. Merrifield didn't trip over Clint, but he made enough of a commotion when he came in to wake him up.

"Bill?"

"Shhhhh," Merrifield said, drawing it out drunkenly, "I don't want to wake Clint. Go to sleep."

He continued on, stumbled into bed, and Clint rolled over and went back to sleep.

• • •

He woke in the morning to the smell of coffee. He opened his eyes and saw Sylvane in the kitchen.

"Coffee?" Sylvane offered.

"Please."

Clint got up and walked to the kitchen table, where he fell heavily into a chair. Sylvane handed him a cup.

"You figure your brother will come back today with Roosevelt?"

"Roosevelt paid for two weeks," Sylvane said. "The two weeks is up today. I guess we'll just have to wait and see."

"Is Merrifield up?"

"No," Sylvane said. "He must have got back real late last night."

"I heard him come in, but I don't know what time it was."

"I've got to ride out and check the stock," Sylvane said. "I guess I'll do it without him."

"Let me finish my coffee," Clint said, "and I'll go with you."

"You work a herd?" Sylvane asked.

"I have in my time."

"That's not part of your reputation."

"No, it's not," Clint said.

"I'll go out and saddle the horses. You need a pony?"

"No," Clint said, "I can work with Duke, but don't try to saddle him. You'll lose a finger."

"Okay," Sylvane said, "I'll be waiting for you in the barn."

"Give me a couple of minutes to wash up and wake up," Clint said. "Is there any water?"

"There's a pump around the side of the house," Sylvane said.

"Okay," Clint said. "See you in a couple of minutes."

Sylvane nodded and left. It had been a few years since Clint had worked with cattle, but it wasn't something you forgot. He finished the coffee and went out to the pump.

When Clint and Sylvane returned, Merrifield was up—sort of. He was awake, but he was sitting at the kitchen table with his head in his hands when they walked in.

"Any coffee left?" Sylvane asked.

"I didn't check."

"You didn't have any?"

"I just got up," Merrifield said, "and this is as far as I got. I was gonna try for the stove next."

"I'll pour it," Sylvane said, as Clint sat across the table from Merrifield.

Sylvane poured three cups and carried them to the table. Merrifield took a mouthful and swallowed gratefully.

"What have you two been up to?"

"Clint helped me with the herd," Sylvane said. "He did your job for you."

"Thanks, Clint," Merrifield said. "I don't think I could have sat a horse this morning."

"Don't mention it. What have you got planned for the rest of the day?"

"I'm gonna move slow, so my head don't fall off."

"You want to head into town?" Sylvane asked Clint. "Talk to the Varney boys?"

"That's what I was thinking," Clint said.

"Why the Varney boys?" Merrifield asked. "Oh, you mean about the game last night?"

"More than that," Sylvane said. "Somebody took a shot at Clint last night when he left the saloon."

"A shot?" Merrifield said. "I think I heard a shot, but I was under Esther at the time." He looked at Clint. "Did you see who it was?"

"No."

"You think it was Zack Varney?"

"That's what I want to find out," Clint said.

"The shot seemed to come from right across the street," Sylvane said.

"Hmm," Merrifield said. "The general store is right across the street."

"Yes, it is," Sylvane said. "I'm gonna ride in with Clint, Bill."

"Fine," Merrifield said. "I can come, too, but you'll have to wait—"

"That's okay," Clint said. "Stay here. Maybe Sylvane's brother and Roosevelt will come back."

"You're right," Merrifield said. "I'll stay here."

Sylvane looked at Clint.

"Just give me a chance to take care of my pony, and then saddle a different horse."

"I'll wait here."

Sylvane nodded and went outside.

"He seems all right, your partner," Clint said.

"For a man who doesn't like people," Merrifield said, "he seems to have taken to you."

"I'm a helluva guy, that's why," Clint said.

"What are you gonna do when you see the Varneys?" Merrifield asked.

"Just ask a few questions," Clint said, "and then give out some advice."

"Marie works in the store," Merrifield said. "I'd like to know what you think of her."

"Why?"

"You said you like smart women."

"And she's smart?"

Merrifield nodded.

"And beautiful."

"Then what's she doing with Varney?"

"I think we talked about that last night," Merrifield said. "I ask myself that question all the time."

"Well," Clint said, "I'll let you know what I think when I get back."

"Watch your back."

Clint headed for the door and said, "I intend to."

THIRTY-SEVEN

When Clint and Sylvane rode into Little Misery, the town was real quiet. It seemed as if everyone was sleeping off a hangover, the way Merrifield had done.

"After we finish with the Varney boys," Sylvane said, "you might want to ride down to the river and take a look at Medora."

"The Marquis' town?" Clint said. "I'd be interested to do that—and I'd be interested to meet this Marquis."

"Maybe I can arrange that," Sylvane said.

They rode up to the general store, dismounted, and tied their horses.

"Want me to come in with you?" Sylvane asked.

Clint shook his head.

"It might be better if you stayed out here," Clint said.

"I can watch your back from here," Sylvane said, "but be careful inside."

173

"I will."

Clint went into the store and stopped short when he saw the woman behind the counter. Merrifield had said she was beautiful, but that word was inadequate to describe her—that is, if this was Marie Varney.

"Can I help you?" she asked. The store was empty, and he was the only customer in sight.

"I—uh, are you—is Zack Varney around?" Clint asked, aware that he was stammering.

"Not right now," she said. "I'm Marie Varney. Do you have some business with my husband?"

He wanted to ask her what she was doing with a man like Zack Varney, but those words wouldn't come out. In fact, no words would come out at the moment.

She had black hair, black as night, and long, down to her shoulders. She was wearing a simple dress that buttoned to her neck, and while she wasn't flaunting it, she couldn't hide the body beneath it. Her skin was pale, her lips very full and sensual, her cheekbones high, her eyes large and luminous, a startling ice-blue.

And those eyes were boring into him now.

"Mister?"

"Uh, my name is Clint Adams. I, uh, saw your husband last night."

"Saw him?" The expression on her face changed. It was no longer inquiring. "I'll bet you're the one who took all his money, am I right?"

"Uh, well—"

"Have you come to give it back?"

"Well, no—"

"I didn't think so. Why are you here, Mr. Adams?"

"Well . . . I just wanted to talk to your husband, Mrs. Varney."

"About what?" she asked.

"Well—"

"Was he a sore loser last night?" she asked. "Don't tell me, I know the answer to that. He's always a sore loser. What did he do?"

"Well—"

"Did he threaten you?" she asked, not letting him get a word in. "That idiot! What did he say?"

"Well . . ." he paused, thinking she was going to interrupt him, but she didn't, so he went on. "Someone took a shot at me last night, outside the saloon."

"Jesus," she said, shaking her head. "Is he that much of an idiot?" He realized she wasn't asking him the question, but herself.

"What about his brother, Len?" Clint asked. "Is he around?"

"No," she said. "Mister, I don't know if my husband is stupid enough to take a shot at you. He's stupid, don't get me wrong, but I don't know if he's that stupid."

"Ma'am," he said, "I just want to talk to him about it, find out if it was him."

"And then what?"

"And then I'd like to convince him not to try it again."

"You don't want to kill him?"

"I don't want to kill anyone," Clint said, "that's the whole point. All I did was sit down to play some poker, and the cards started coming to me. I don't think I should be shot at for that, do you?"

"Definitely not," she said, shaking her head and making a chopping motion with her hand, "I agree. What you should probably do is just beat him to a pulp."

"Excuse me?"

"He deserves that, at least."

"Ma'am," he said patiently, "I just want to talk to him."

"Well . . . he should be back in a little while. He and his brother went off . . . somewhere." She waved her hand. "They're always going off somewhere and leaving me to do the work. For instance, I've got a keg of nails in the back room that has to come out here. Do you think either of them would stay around to help me?"

"A keg of nails?"

She nodded.

"I can help."

"Really?" she asked. "You wouldn't mind?"

"Not at all."

Suddenly, her look turned shrewd.

"And what are you going to want in return?"

"I beg your pardon?"

"It's my experience that men never offer their help unless they want something in return."

"Then I think you've been hanging around with the wrong men."

"Do you think I don't know that?" she asked. "All right, come on. Those nails are back here. . . ."

THIRTY-EIGHT

Clint struggled with the keg of nails and then finally tilted it and wheeled it out into the front.

"You haven't worked in a store before, have you?" she asked.

"No, ma'am," Clint said. "I'm afraid I haven't ever been a clerk."

"No," she said, standing back and folding her arms. Her breasts were large, so she had to fold her arms beneath them. "You don't look like a clerk. What did you say your name was?"

"Clint Adams."

She frowned.

"I'm afraid I wasn't listening earlier," she said. "I know your reputation."

"Does that mean I can't help you anymore?"

"You want to do more?"

"Why not?" he said. "I've got nothing else to do, and I can help you while I wait for your husband to come back."

"Well," she said, "if that's what you really want to do."

"Just let me tell my friend outside that I'll be staying."

She craned her neck to look out the window.

"Is that Sylvane Ferris?"

"Yes."

"Tell him I said hello."

"I'll be right back."

Clint went outside and told Sylvane that he was going to stay and wait for Varney to come back.

"Want me to wait with you?"

"No," Clint said, "that won't be necessary. I'm just going to help Mrs. Varney with a few things while I'm waiting."

"You're going to help Marie?"

"That's right," Clint said. "By the way, she said to tell you 'hello.' "

"Well," Sylvane said, "tell her I said 'hi' back—and you'd better watch your back."

"I know—"

"No," Sylvane said, "even more than before."

"Why?"

"Because there's one thing about Zack Varney that's worse than him being a sore loser."

"What's that?"

"He's jealous," Sylvane said. "When he gets back and finds you helping his wife—"

"Why shouldn't I help her?" Clint asked. "He's not

around to do it. And why should he be jealous just because I'm helping around the store?''

"Have you ever had a wife as beautiful as Marie Varney?''

"I've never had a wife.''

Sylvane frowned.

"Why are you doing this, Clint?''

"What do you mean?''

"I mean, what do you expect to get in return?''

"That's what she asked me,'' Clint said, "and the answer is the same—nothing.''

"Oh, come on,'' Sylvane said. "She's a very beautiful woman.''

"So?''

"And you're going to help her just to be . . . help-ful?''

"That's right,'' Clint said. "Don't you think a man can help a woman without wanting something in return?''

"No,'' Sylvane said.

"Why not?''

"Because men aren't like that.''

"Well, I am.''

"Okay, fine. Listen, I'll be at Big-Mouthed Bob's if you need me. Just be careful.''

"I'm always careful, Sylvane,'' Clint said.

"And have a good time.'' Sylvane leered, then headed for the saloon.

"I will not!'' Clint called after him.

THIRTY-NINE

For about an hour Clint learned what it was like to be a clerk in a general store. What he did was mostly heavy lifting that Marie Varney couldn't have done, and he climbed up on a ladder a few times to reach something on a top shelf. He also drew looks from some customers who came in who were probably wondering who he was, and where Marie's husband was.

While he was there they also talked, and he discovered that what Merrifield had said about her was correct. She was as smart as she was beautiful.

"Marie?"

"Yes?"

"I think we've known each other long enough for me to ask you a personal question."

"Well, sure," she said. "After all, it's been . . . what? An hour? Go ahead and ask."

"How did someone like you end up here?" he asked.

"You mean, how did I end up with somebody like Zack Varney?"

"I guess that's what I mean."

She leaned on the counter and said, "You know, a day doesn't go by I don't ask myself that same question."

Before she could answer it, though, Zack Varney came through the front door, followed by his brother Len. The brothers were both talking at the same time, maybe even arguing, but they both stopped short when they saw Clint Adams behind the counter with Marie.

"What the hell—" Zack Varney started, but his brother put his hand on his arm to stop him.

"What are you doing here?" Len Varney asked.

"He was looking for you boys," Marie said, not giving Clint a chance to reply, "and decided to stay around and wait for you."

"Why's he behind the counter?" Zack asked.

"Because he was nice enough to help me around here while you two were off doing God knows what," she said. "There were some chores that needed to be done . . . by a man."

Her emphasis on the word "man" did not go unnoticed by any of the three men in the store.

Zack Varney squinted at his wife.

"How long's he been here?"

"About an hour."

"An hour?" he said. "And what have you two been doin' for an hour?"

"Zack," Len said, and his brother fell silent. "That right, mister? You wanted to see us?"

"Mostly," Clint said, "I wanted to see your brother Zack."

"And why's that?"

Clint came around the counter and faced both brothers.

"Somebody took a shot at me last night, as I was leaving the saloon."

"Are you sayin' it was me?" Zack demanded.

"I thought I'd come and ask you if it was you, Zack," Clint said.

"Why would I take a shot at you?"

"Well, you were pretty upset about losing your money," Clint pointed out.

"And you thought I'd shoot you to get it back?"

"I don't know you, Zack," Clint said. "I don't know what you'd do. I asked your brother, here, last night what you might do, and he said he didn't know. Of course, he never told me you were brothers."

"It never came up," Len Varney said, "not during the whole game."

"No," Clint said, "I guess it didn't. We didn't exactly exchange names, did we?"

"No, we didn't," Len said. "In fact, we didn't get your name."

"It's Adams," Clint said, "Clint Adams."

That stopped both brothers short, and Clint decided to give them time to recover.

"Adams?" Len Varney finally said.

"That's right."

Zack rubbed his hand over his face.

"We didn't know," Len said.

"What's the difference?" Clint asked. "Are you saying you wouldn't have taken a shot at me if you knew who I was?''

''I didn't—I never said I took a shot at you,'' Zack said.

''That's right, you didn't,'' Clint said. ''So let's just say that whether you did or not last night, it wouldn't be a good idea to try it in the future. How's that?''

''We got no reason to shoot at you,'' Len Varney said.

''Fine,'' Clint said, ''let's keep it that way.''

He turned to look at Marie.

''Thanks for letting me wait, Mrs. Varney.''

''And thank you for your help, Mr. Adams.''

''It was my pleasure.'' He turned back to the brothers. ''Excuse me.''

They spread apart far enough for him to slide between them and head for the door. Zack started to say something. Whether it was to his brother or to his wife, Clint didn't know because Len shushed him immediately. He probably wanted to wait until Clint was further out of earshot before they started talking.

Which suited Clint fine. He crossed the street and headed for Big-Mouthed Bob's.

FORTY

"There he is," Sylvane said as Clint entered the saloon.

It was clear that he and Bob had been talking about him.

"I thought you'd be over there a lot longer," Sylvane said as Bob put a beer on the bar.

"The Varney boys came back a little while ago." Clint picked up the beer with a nod of thanks to Bob.

"What was that like?" Sylvane asked.

"We talked."

"That's all?"

"I introduced myself."

"Oh," Sylvane said, "you didn't exchange names last night. They didn't know who you are?"

"I didn't know who you were until Sylvane told me a little while ago," Bob said. "Seems to me those boys

would have been pretty stupid to shoot at you, knowin'
who you was. Now that they know, I don't think you'll
have to worry about either one of them.''

"If it was them," Sylvane said. "Did they admit it?"

"No," Clint said, "but I'm pretty sure it was Zack.
He seems to be the stupid one. Even his wife told me
that."

"She should know," Sylvane said. "I don't know
what she's doing with him."

"She and I were talking about that."

"You were?"

"She was about to answer that very question when
they walked in."

"Marie Varney is the most beautiful woman I ever
saw," Bob said, a dreamy look on his face. "If I could
get a gal in here who looked like her . . ."

"Your gals are good-looking enough, Bob," Sylvane
said.

Bob shook his head.

"Not like her."

"There aren't that many women like Marie Varney,
Bob," Clint said, "and the ones there are you won't
find working in a saloon."

"Sure as hell not in Big-Mouthed Bob's in Little Misery," Bob agreed, nodding.

"You gonna see her again?" Sylvane asked.

"Why would I?" Clint asked.

"Well," Sylvane said, "you asked her a question,
didn't you?"

"Well, yeah—"

"And you didn't get an answer, did you?"

"No, but—"

"Seems to me that's reason enough."

"As if a man needed a reason to want to see her again," Bob said.

"Didn't you say something about showing me the town across the river?" Clint asked Sylvane. "What's it called?"

"Medora," Sylvane said. "Yeah, we can ride by the river and take a look."

"Don't tell me if he's built himself a saloon," Bob said to them. "I don't want to know it. The way people are leavin' this place, I sure don't need no competition."

"We won't tell you," Sylvane said.

"We're not even going to cross the river," Clint said. "I'm just curious enough to take a look from this side."

Clint and Sylvane went outside. Across the street Clint caught a quick movement just inside the general store.

"Did you see that?" Sylvane asked.

"I did."

"Somebody was watching," Sylvane said.

"I saw."

"You don't think those boys would plan something stupid now that they know who you are, do you?"

"They might plan something stupid," Clint said, "*because* they know who I am. It's happened before."

"That seems *real* stupid," Sylvane said.

"You might want to get out of the line of fire, Sylvane," Clint said.

"I reckon I'll take my chances, Clint," Sylvane said. "Come on. I'll show you Medora."

They rode to the river, and Clint saw the buildings on the other side. It didn't look quite like a town yet, but then did Little Missouri?

"See that chimney?" Sylvane asked.

There was a chimney that stood well above every other structure, so he couldn't help but see it.

"Yes."

"That's his slaughterhouse."

"Now this is something you and Bill don't agree on, isn't it?" Clint said.

"What's that?"

"You think the Marquis' plan is viable, don't you?" Clint asked.

"Yes, I do."

"Well, if that's the case," Clint said, "instead of getting edged out of this valley, maybe you can work with him. Bring him your cattle, as well."

Sylvane shook his head.

"Bill would never go for it," Sylvane said.

"Are there others around here who won't?"

"Plenty," Sylvane said. "The Marquis got himself a little feud going with three men in particular a while back."

"What happened?"

Sylvane looked at Clint, then said, "Come on. I'll tell you the story on the way back home."

FORTY-ONE

"Their names are Frank O'Donald, Riley Luffsey, and Dutch Wannegan."

"What do they have against the Marquis?"

"I don't rightly know how it started, Clint," Sylvane said. "The way I heard it, the Marquis offered O'Donald work, and O'Donald turned him down. He said he preferred to live on what he made huntin' and trappin'."

"Nothing wrong with that."

"Well, O'Donald is also not fond of E. G. Paddock, and Paddock has thrown in with the Frenchman."

"Okay."

"Well, again, the way I heard it, O'Donald was on his way home to the shack he shared with Luffsey and Wannegan when he came across a fence blocking his path. He tore it down; the Marquis put it back up. After that every time O'Donald, or Luffsey, or Wannegan would come across that fence they'd tear it down.''

''And the Marquis would put it back?''

''Right.''

''Then what happened?''

''Well, the Marquis, he decided to push it. He started a rumor that he was going to jump claim on that shack the three men were sharing. They sent back word that whoever tried to jump them would jump right into his grave.''

''And what happened?''

''It came to a head in June. Let me see if I can make this short. The three men came to town, started drinking Bob's Forty-Mile Red-eye and sayin' they were gonna shoot the Marquis. The Frenchman got on a train and took it to Mandan. That's a hundred and fifty miles away.''

''The nearest sheriff, if I remember what someone told me last night.''

''He was apparently told that if fired upon, he should fire back. Well, he returned, and two days later somebody took a shot at him. They missed, but the Marquis sent a telegram to the sheriff, who arrived on the next train.''

''To find what?''

''To find O'Donald, Luffsey, and Wannegan waiting at the station, armed. When he told them they were under arrest, they refused to be taken. They turned and left the station, and . . .''

''And what?''

''And walked into an ambush,'' Sylvane said. ''They were shot up and surrendered, except for Luffsey, who died.''

''What happened then?''

"The Marquis, Paddock, and a couple of other men came out of hiding and they were all arrested, except for Paddock, who didn't have a gun."

"Was there a trial?"

"There was, and the Marquis was found not guilty. After all, the men were technically under arrest, and fleeing."

"What happened then?" Clint asked, as the house came into view.

"Well, the word went out that if the Marquis de Mores ever returned here he would be lynched."

"But he returned."

Sylvane nodded.

"And no one dared lay a hand on him. His town continued to be built, and his fences continued to go up."

"That's quite a story," Clint said. "What about O'Donald and Wannegan?"

"They left. Nobody's ever seen them again."

"So everyone assumes they left," Clint said.

Sylvane looked at him.

"You think they were killed?"

Clint shrugged.

"If you say they left, they left."

Sylvane frowned.

"What are your feelings about the Marquis, Sylvane?"

"I don't have any," the man said. "Those three were no friends of mine, and he hasn't tried to fence off any of our land—yet."

"What will happen if he does?"

"I guess we'll find out then, won't we?" Sylvane asked.

As they rode up to the house they heard some horses in the barn being particularly noisy.

"That sounds like Joe's pinto," Sylvane said.

"Your brother?"

Sylvane nodded.

"That horse is ornery and kicks up a fuss for no reason. That usually starts the rest of them. Let's go right up to the house and see if he's back."

They did so, dismounting and entering the house.

Clint was immediately grabbed in a bear hug and practically lifted off his feet.

"Clint Adams!" Teddy Roosevelt shouted in his ear. "By God, it is you!"

"Put me down, Teddy," Clint said. "I can't breathe."

"I couldn't believe it when Merrifield told me," Roosevelt said. He released Clint and stepped back. "Gentlemen, this is the deadliest pool player it's ever been my misfortune to come across—and the best friend."

"What's pool?" Merrifield asked.

"You must be Joe Ferris," Clint said to the fifth man in the room, "Sylvane's brother."

"That's me," Joe said. He stepped forward and shook hands.

"Teddy," Clint said, "you're looking well."

"I feel great," Roosevelt said enthusiastically. "I love this country."

"Did you find any buffalo?"

"No," Roosevelt said. "But I saw some beautiful country, and we even saw some Indians."

"Sioux," Joe said. "They didn't bother us, so we didn't bother them."

"It was all so exciting," Roosevelt said.

"How's your father?"

"He's well," Teddy said, "the whole family is well."

"And are Delvecchio and Anson still working for you?" Clint asked.

"Indeed they are," Teddy said. "When my father gives his word, he keeps it. Those two will be employed for as long as they want."

"That's good."

The other three men in the room were less than excited by the reunion and were starting to look bored.

"I smell something cooking," Sylvane Ferris said.

"Dinner," Merrifield said. "The least I could do after this morning."

"I'll take care of the horses," Sylvane said, "and Clint and his friend can catch up."

"I'll help you," Joe said to his brother. "I've got some things to tell you."

Clint wondered if these things were about Teddy Roosevelt. He figured that the western men would find the New York politician odd, to say the least.

"Why don't you two sit down," Merrifield said to Roosevelt and Clint, "and I'll pour you some coffee."

"Bully," Roosevelt said, grabbing Clint's arm and pulling him toward the table. "I want to hear everything that's happened to you since I saw you last."

"Everything?" Clint asked.

"Everything."

FORTY-TWO

It took two cups of coffee to bring Roosevelt up to date on what Clint had been doing—and that was because Clint left a lot out.

The Ferris brothers came back in and had some coffee, as well, also listening to Clint's stories. Since they were seasoned Westerners, Clint thought they'd be bored by what he was telling Roosevelt, but in fact they seemed to become very interested, especially when he talked about New Orleans.

"I ain't never been to New Orleans," Joe Ferris said. "Never seen the Mississippi."

"I haven't either," Sylvane said.

"Saw the Mississippi once," Merrifield said, "but it was up north a ways, never down south."

"That's what I meant," Joe said. "I'd really like to go to New Orleans."

"You should," Roosevelt said. "I've been there. It's a wonderful city."

"Someday, maybe," Sylvane said, "when we get things rolling here."

"And speaking of getting things rolling," Roosevelt said, "I understand you and your partner are looking for another partner."

Sylvane and Merrifield exchanged a glance.

"Maybe," Sylvane said.

"Well, if you are," Roosevelt said, "I've got some money to invest. You just have to say the word."

Again, Sylvane and his partner exchanged a glance, and it seemed to go unspoken that Sylvane should continue to do the talking.

"How much money are we talking about?" Sylvane asked.

"Well," Teddy said, "I think that's something we can discuss . . . perhaps after dinner?"

"That sounds good," Sylvane said. He looked at his partner. "After dinner."

"After dinner's good," Merrifield said. "I'll get it."

"And during dinner," Clint said to Teddy, "you can tell me what you've been up to for the past five months."

"Ah," Roosevelt said, "successes and failures both, I'm afraid. I am to become a father soon, but circumstances cause me to be away from home for that momentous occasion."

"That's too bad," Sylvane said. "Seems a fella ought to be there when his child is born."

"My health," Roosevelt said, touching his chest.

"The doctor thought this trip would do me some good—and by God, he was right. I feel wonderful."

"Let's talk about it some more, Teddy," Clint said, "over dinner."

FORTY-THREE

After dinner Clint left the table and the house to allow Teddy to talk his business with Merrifield and Sylvane Ferris. Joe stayed. Clint didn't know if Joe Ferris was a partner or not, but he was Sylvane's brother, so he was entitled to stay.

Clint went outside to take a walk around the grounds, and he ended up in the barn brushing Duke. That's where he was when Teddy Roosevelt came walking in.

"Is your business done?" Clint asked.

"Yes," Roosevelt said. "I am a rancher now."

"I didn't know you wanted to be a rancher, Teddy," Clint said. "You never mentioned it."

Roosevelt frowned. Clint noticed for the first time that Roosevelt's Western clothes, though covered with dirt and dust, were expensive. They were probably purchased in New York before he left. He also noticed that

199

he was wearing a brand-new gun belt and a new Colt on his hip.

"I don't think I ever thought of it back then," Teddy said. "What do you think of my decision?"

Clint shrugged.

"It's your money, to invest in any way you wish."

"Well," Roosevelt said, "one of the first things to do will be to expand the house."

"Why?"

"Because I intend to have my own room," Teddy said. "Just because we're living in the West doesn't mean we have to rough it. Not when I have the money to fix the place up. We also need a guest room, for when friends like you come to stay."

Somehow, Clint didn't think that these were the things Sylvane and Merrifield had in mind when they were looking for a partner with money.

"How about a new barn?" Clint asked.

"Yes, that, too."

"And a corral."

"Of course. My partners have laid all of that out for me. But there are other concerns, as well."

"Such as?"

"This French fellow."

"The Marquis de Mores?"

"Yes," Roosevelt said. "I want to go and see him, and I was wondering if you would come with me."

"What do you want to see him about?" Clint stopped brushing Duke, set the brush down, and turned to face Roosevelt.

"Well, he seems to be the power around here at the moment," Teddy said. "I understand he's building his own town, and a slaughterhouse, and that he's buying up land all around us.''

''So?''

''I want to find out what his intentions are.''

Roosevelt sounded like a father who was wondering about his daughter's suitor.

''I think his intentions are pretty clear,'' Clint said. ''He wants to become richer than he already is.''

''Well, I want to find out if he intends to bother us.''

''And how are you going to find this out?'' Clint asked. ''Just ask him?''

''I thought that was how I'd start,'' Teddy said, ''but I think I'll need someone to go in there with me.''

''You have partners.''

Roosevelt shook his head.

''I want you. Will you do it?''

''Of course I'll do it, Teddy,'' Clint said. ''When?''

''Tomorrow.''

''All right,'' Clint said, ''tomorrow it is.''

''By the way,'' Teddy asked, ''what are the chances of you becoming a partner?''

''I don't think Sylvane, for one, wants any more partners.''

''That's silly,'' Teddy said. ''I can convince him.''

''You just met him a couple of hours ago.''

''I'm a good judge of men.''

''There's no need,'' Clint said. ''I really don't have any desire to become a rancher.''

''All right, then,'' Teddy said. ''When shall we go and see this Marquis?''

''How about right after breakfast?''

''Bully,'' Teddy said. ''I'm going to sleep here tonight. I stayed at that hotel in town when I arrived, and it was awful. All I got was a cot in a room full of cots.''

"You can take the floor in the main room of the house," Clint said. "I'll sleep out here."

"In the barn?"

"I'll be comfortable on a bed of hay," Clint assured him.

"Well, all right," Teddy said. "I'm very excited about this, Clint. I love the West, and now I'm a part of it."

"Congratulations, Teddy," Clint said. "I hope it turns out to be all you want it to be."

"Oh, it will," the politician said. "Good night."

"Good night, Teddy."

As Roosevelt left the barn Clint turned and patted Duke's neck.

"Well, big boy, it looks like you've got a roommate tonight."

FORTY-FOUR

In the morning Clint awoke refreshed. He'd actually had a better night's sleep in the barn than he'd had the previous night in the house. When he got up to the house all three men were already awake and Sylvane was making breakfast.

"Understand you and Teddy are going to see the Marquis today," Merrifield said.

"That's right."

"Good," Merrifield said. "Maybe you can keep him from trying to crowd us out of this valley."

"That's what we're going to do," Roosevelt said. "Now that I am a partner here, no one is going to crowd me out."

Sylvane dished out eggs and bacon, as well as biscuits, and poured everyone a cup of coffee before sitting himself to eat.

"Well," Teddy said, "at least I know I won't starve out here. You're quite a cook, Sylvane, every bit as good as your brother said."

Clint looked around then and realized for the first time that Joe was missing.

"Where is your brother?" he asked Sylvane.

"He left last night."

"I didn't hear his horse."

"He walked. Said he didn't want to wake you or his horse."

"What?" Clint asked. "Why not?"

"Don't you know?"

"No."

"From the time you went into the barn, did you hear his horse?"

"Well, no . . ."

"He thinks you have some calming effect on the horse," Sylvane explained, "and he didn't want to take him out of the barn."

"That's silly," Clint said. "Maybe the horse was just tired."

Clint remembered looking over at the pinto and won-dering why Sylvane had said the animal was so ornery.

"So he walked to town?" Clint asked.

"Joe walks a lot," Sylvane said.

"He walked a lot while I was out with him," Roo-sevelt said. "I've never seen such a tireless man."

Clint shook his head and decided not to question it any more. The Ferris brothers were sort of an odd pair—although certainly not as odd as the Varney boys.

Thinking about the Varney brothers made Clint think about Marie Varney. She couldn't be happy living with those two men. Why didn't she just leave?

After breakfast Roosevelt was raring to go.

"Teddy," Sylvane said, because that's what Roosevelt had told his new partners to call him, "there's no guarantee that the Marquis will see you, you know. He's got men around him all the time, since that incident in June."

"Joe told me about that," Teddy said. "I think I can get him to see me, though. After all, I did borrow a gun from Mr. Paddock."

"E. G. Paddock?" Clint asked.

"That's right. He was kind enough to lend me a weapon more conducive to buffalo hunting. My Sharps had a broken hammer, and my Winchester was too light."

"Then through Paddock you can get to de Mores."

"Maybe," Sylvane said. "With Paddock you never know."

"We'll ride over to see him, to return the gun I borrowed," Roosevelt said, "and I will ask him to introduce me to the Frenchman. I think I can get him to do it."

"I hope you can," Merrifield said. "Once we start expanding our operation we don't need to get any trouble from him."

"Don't worry," Teddy said. "I'll make our intentions very clear to the man. Ready, Clint?"

"I'm ready, Teddy."

The two men went outside and saddled their horses. Clint was impressed with how easily Roosevelt accomplished this, and swung into the saddle. It was obvious that Roosevelt was an accomplished horseman.

They rode into town and did not stop. Roosevelt remembered the way to Paddock's cabin, and along the way he and Clint traded what information they had each gotten from one of the Ferris brothers. As it turned out, they were both pretty much in possession of the same information.

Except that Clint knew nothing of Paddock.

"An odd man, to say the least," Teddy said. "He wears two guns and is a decidedly villainous-looking man—yet his manner was pleasant."

"Maybe you just bring that out in people, Teddy," Clint said.

Roosevelt laughed.

"The people who know me in New York would not agree with you, my friend."

They rode a bit further past town and then Roosevelt said, "There is the cabin. A modest abode for a man who once controlled this valley."

"Control he has since given up to the Marquis, eh?" Clint asked.

"The Marquis arrived here with fresh money, Clint," Roosevelt said. "He is investing quite a bit of it to build a town, and a slaughterhouse, and a grand house on a hill overlooking everything. When a man flashes that much money, he pretty much gains control of those around him, as well."

"Well," Clint said, "let's go and see if your friend Paddock can get us in to see this great man."

FORTY-FIVE

Clint and Roosevelt rode up to the cabin owned by
E. G. Paddock and dismounted.

"He was most gracious the first time I met him,"
Roosevelt said as they walked up to the door. "Generous, as well."

"I can't wait to meet him," Clint said.

Roosevelt led the way and knocked on the door.
When the door was opened Clint knew what Roosevelt
had meant when he said Paddock was "villainous-
looking."

The man standing in the door was a tall, grizzled-
looking man with pale eyes, a black goatee, and a Man-
darin mustache hanging down either side of his face,
almost past his chin. He wore a pair of Colt revolvers
on his slender hips.

"Mr. Paddock," Teddy said, "I've come to return the rifle you so generously loaned me."

"It's Mr. Roosevelt, isn't it?" Paddock asked, even though he was looking past Roosevelt at Clint.

Clint had been told that Paddock had been a gambler and guide, as well as a speculator in hunting rights along the river. The man stood, however, like someone who knew how to handle the weapons he was wearing.

"That's right."

Reluctantly, the man took his eyes off of Clint.

"And did you manage to find any buffalo?" he asked, accepting the weapon back from Roosevelt.

"I'm afraid not."

"That's too bad. Is there anything else I can do for you, then?"

"As a matter of fact, there is," Roosevelt said. "Perhaps we could come in and discuss it?"

"Well," Paddock said, "before I let a man into my home I generally like to know his name." He looked past Roosevelt at Clint again.

"I'm sorry," Teddy said. "Let me introduce my friend, Clint Adams."

"Adams?"

"That's right."

"The Gunsmith."

Clint simply nodded.

"And what brings you to Little Misery, Mr. Adams?" Paddock asked. "I wouldn't think a man . . . a man like you would find much here to interest you."

"I have friends here," Clint said.

"Of which I am one," Roosevelt said.

"Who are the others?" Paddock asked.

"Bill Merrifield."

Paddock nodded.

"I know Mr. Merrifield."

"May we come in, then?" Roosevelt asked.

"Of course," Paddock said, backing away from the door. "Please come in."

Roosevelt and Clint entered the house, and Paddock closed the door behind them. It was small and modestly furnished, but Paddock's clothes—and his guns—spoke of money. Clint wondered what the man did with most of his money.

He turned to face Paddock and asked, "Do you always wear your guns in your house?"

Paddock smiled, giving his face an even more evil cast.

"I didn't know who was at the door, Mr. Adams," he said. "I'm sure you of all people can understand that."

"Yes," Clint said, "I can."

Paddock looked at Roosevelt.

"Can I offer you a drink?"

"No, thank you," Roosevelt said. "We really only have one request of you, Mr. Paddock."

"And what would that be?"

"We would like you to introduce us to the Marquis de Mores."

"Really?" Paddock asked. "Why?"

"I have recently become a partner in the Maltese Cross Ranch," Roosevelt said.

"Isn't that the ranch owned by Bill Merrifield and Sylvane Ferris?"

"That's right."

Paddock looked at Clint.

"And are you also a partner in this ranch?"

"No," Clint said, "I'm not. Like I said, I'm just a friend."

"I see." Paddock turned his attention to Roosevelt. "Well, Mr. Roosevelt, that still doesn't tell me why you want to meet the Marquis."

"It is my understanding that he holds the power around here," Roosevelt said.

"Who told you that? Ferris? Merrifield?" Paddock looked mildly annoyed. "What do they know about power? I mean, real power?"

"They know that you held it," Clint said, "until the Marquis arrived."

Paddock looked at Clint and then impressed him by not losing his temper. Instead, he took the time to light a long, thin, brown cigar before replying.

"The Marquis and I work together," he said simply. He would allow Clint and Roosevelt to draw their own conclusions.

"If that's the case," Roosevelt said, "then you can get us in to see him."

"Why should I?" Paddock asked.

"Maybe," Clint said, "just to show us that you can."

FORTY-SIX

For a moment Clint thought that he had played Paddock all wrong. He and Roosevelt exchanged a glance while Paddock worked on his cigar. When he was satisfied with the glow on the end of it, he looked at the other two men.

"I'll arrange it."

"Good," Roosevelt said. "Very good."

"For tomorrow."

"Oh, I'd rather it be today," Roosevelt said. "I'd like to get this settled as soon as possible."

"What is there to settle?"

Roosevelt looked at Clint.

"I think Mr. Roosevelt would prefer to tell that to you . . . *and* to your . . . partner, together."

Paddock seemed to like Clint's use of the word "partner."

211

"All right," Paddock said. "In two hours."

"Where?" Roosevelt asked.

"In Medora."

Roosevelt looked at Clint for clarification.

"The town he's building across the river," Clint said.

"Oh, of course," Roosevelt said, "his town. Very well. That's an excellent place."

"You fellas will have to amuse yourselves for that time, and then ride into Medora."

"We'll find a way," Clint assured him.

"We very much appreciate your help, Mr. Paddock," Roosevelt said. "And once again, thank you for the use of the gun."

"Don't mention it," Paddock said. "I'm just sorry you didn't actually get to use it."

"We will see you in two hours, then," Roosevelt said.

"I'll see you to the door."

He let them out and then closed the door behind them, very gently.

"You touched a nerve," Roosevelt said as they walked to the horses.

"He hid it very well."

"Nevertheless, you touched it. You played him just right. You're a remarkable judge of men, Clint."

"This is the West, Teddy," Clint said, "where I'm at home. I know how these men think."

"Hmm," Roosevelt said as they mounted up, "I don't think your Western mores will work on the Frenchman, though, do you?"

Clint smiled at Roosevelt and said, "Maybe I'll just leave the Marquis to you, Teddy."

"He does sound like the type of man I routinely handle in New York,'' Roosevelt said, ''but I guess time will tell.''

''We'll know,'' Clint said, ''in two hours. Until then, let me introduce you to Big-Mouthed Bob.''

''Oh, I met Bob when I first arrived,'' Roosevelt said. ''Did you try his Forty-Mile Red-eye?''

''No,'' Clint said, ''I was warned away from it.''

''Ah,'' Roosevelt said, ''I didn't have that advantage. Foul stuff! Come on, I'll buy you a beer.''

''Sounds good to me.''

As they rode away from Paddock's home toward town Roosevelt asked, ''Do you suppose they have a pool table anywhere in town?''

FORTY-SEVEN

Clint and Roosevelt rode back to Little Misery, left their horses in front of the saloon, and went in to keep Big-Mouthed Bob company.

After they left E. G. Paddock's, the man watched them ride away, then left the house and mounted his own horse. He rode across the river to Medora and found Antoine-Amedee-Marie-Vincent-Amat Manca de Valombrosa, Marquis de Mores supervising the finishing touches on his slaughterhouse.

"Ah, *mon ami* Paddock," de Mores said.

The Frenchman was very dark and very handsome, with the eyes of an eagle and a carefully waxed mustache. His bearing bespoke both military and royal lineage, dating back to thirteenth-century Spain.

"It is beautiful, no?" de Mores asked, indicating the slaughterhouse.

"Yes, it is," Paddock said. Although his association with the Frenchman had certainly lined his pockets, and would continue to do so, it irked him that the man was at least fifteen years younger than he was, perhaps even more.

"And what brings you out this early, my friend?" the Marquis asked.

"The Maltese Cross Ranch."

De Mores frowned.

"What of it?" he asked. "Is that not—how do you say the names?"

"Merrifield and Ferris," Paddock said.

"Yes, just so, that is their ranch, no?"

"Yes."

"And what is the problem? We will not have to deal with them for some time yet. I am still acquiring the land around them."

"I realize that," Paddock said, "but I received a visit from their partner today."

The Frenchman turned and regarded Paddock with his dark eyes.

"Partner? What partner?"

"A fella named Roosevelt," Paddock said.

"Do I know this Roosevelt?"

"No," Paddock said, "he's not from around here."

"Where is he from?"

"New York City."

"Ah." The Frenchman's eyes lit up. "A civilized man. Perhaps a chess player?"

"I don't know," Paddock said, "maybe you can ask him."

"Am I to be meeting this civilized gentleman from New York City?" the Marquis asked.

"He wants to meet you."

"And he came to you to arrange it?"

"Yes."

"Why?"

"He knows of our, eh, association."

"I see."

The Frenchman stared at his slaughterhouse for a few moments, then turned to Paddock and said, "Come to my house."

"When?"

"Now," the Frenchman said, and turned and walked to a buggy that was waiting nearby.

Paddock watched as the man climbed into the buggy and drove it away toward his hilltop house, then shook his head, mounted his horse, and followed.

When they reached the house there was a man there to take the Marquis' horse and buggy, and also to care for Paddock's horse.

"Come inside," the Frenchman said.

Paddock followed the man up the stairs and into the house. As usual, Paddock felt as if he were entering a high-class bordello, for this was the style in which the Frenchman had chosen to decorate his home.

Not only were the furnishings—much of them in red—plush and expensive, but at that very moment a naked girl was coming down the stairs from the second floor. Paddock was always surprised at how many women de Mores kept in his home, and at the fact that he seemed to keep them naked—and they didn't mind.

This one was small, petite even, with tiny breasts topped with pink nipples. Her hair was very black, cut like a man's, and the bush between her legs was . . . well, very bushy.

"Ah, Denise, my love," the Frenchman said.

He opened his arms, and as she came off the last step she ran into his embrace. He closed his arms around her, kissed her hungrily—a kiss, Paddock noted, she returned passionately—and then she simply remained in his embrace while he ran his hands over her hips and thighs and her taut, almost boyish buttocks. He also slid his hand between them and caressed her between her legs briefly.

Paddock knew how her skin felt, for on one of his first nights there he and the Frenchman had drank until they were drunk, and then the man had offered him his choice of three women who were in the house at the time. Paddock had chosen Denise. The girl had been incredible in bed, inventive to the point of embarrassing Paddock, and since then the two had not exchanged a word, and hardly a glance.

"Where are you off to, *mon cheri*?" the Marquis asked.

"I am hungry," she said. "I was going to raid your kitchen."

"Ah, well, then," he said, releasing her, "don't let me stop you. I have some business to take care of, anyway. I will see you later."

She waved to him, a waggle of the fingers of her right hand, and then trotted off to the kitchen.

"A lovely, charming creature," the Marquis said.

"Yes."

The other man sighed.

"It is a shame I must send her away."

"Why?"

The Marquis looked at Paddock and said, "I have grown tired of her, I am afraid."

Paddock had nothing to say to that, although it did occur to him—however briefly—to ask if he could have the girl. He imagined her running around naked in his house all the time, but then shook his head to dispel the thought.

"Come," de Mores said, "we will talk in my office and you will tell me more of this man Roosevelt, from New York City."

As they entered the office, which was furnished in a much more sedate fashion, Paddock said, "There's someone else involved, as well."

"Another partner?" the Marquis asked, seating himself behind a huge cherry wood desk he'd had brought over from France.

"Not exactly," Paddock said, sitting across from the man.

"What then, hmm? Don't make me drag it out of you, *mon ami*."

"Clint Adams."

De Mores sat back and folded his hands in his lap.

"What is a Clint Adams?"

"He's also known as the Gunsmith."

The Frenchman frowned.

"Now that name I have heard."

"I'm sure you've been in this country long enough to have heard it, yes."

"Some sort of legend of the West, hmm?"

"Something like that."

"And why is he here?"

"He's friends with the Maltese Cross people," Paddock said, "and he came with this Roosevelt fella to see me."

"Ah," the Marquis said, "so if I agree to meet with Mr. Roosevelt, then this Gunsmith fellow would come along, as well?"

"I'm sure of it."

"Well, then, set it up, my friend," the Marquis said. "By all means."

"They want it to be today."

"Bring them here, then."

"When?"

De Mores spread his arms and said, "Now. Go and get them. I am ready to entertain them. Where are they?"

"Waiting in town."

"Then get them and bring them here within the hour."

"All right," Paddock said, standing up, "but I want to be here when you talk to them."

"Of course," the Frenchman said, "and you will be wearing both of your six-guns, eh? To intimidate this Gunsmith? You Americans and your legends."

Paddock left the Frenchman's house thinking what little chance there was of intimidating a man like Clint Adams, no matter how many guns you wore.

FORTY-EIGHT

Clint and Roosevelt were enjoying a cold beer each, listening to Big-Mouthed Bob tell stories about his Forty-Mile Red-eye and what it did to people, when E. G. Paddock came walking into the place.

"Mr. Paddock," Roosevelt greeted, "come and join us for a cold beer."

"I think I will," Paddock said. "I'm really dry from talking with the Marquis."

Bob had a beer up on the bar by the time Paddock reached them.

"Did he agree to see us?" Roosevelt asked.

"He did," Paddock said, "but it took a lot of persuading on my part."

"Excellent," Roosevelt said. "I'd wager you can be a very persuasive fellow when you want to be."

"Well," Paddock lied, hoisting the beer, "I had to be

221

today, but it's fine. He'll see you within the hour.''

"That is excellent," Roosevelt said, looking at Clint. "Isn't it?"

"Excellent," Clint said. "Does that include me, Mr. Paddock?"

"Oh, yes," Paddock said, "he's looking forward to meeting one of our Western legends, he said."

"Well, whatever the reason," Roosevelt said, "I'm pleased that he has agreed to see us. Shall we go?"

"I think we can take the time to finish these beers," Paddock said. "Also, I think I should warn you about a few things."

"Like what?" Roosevelt asked.

"The Marquis is sort of a strange man."

"In what way?"

"We'll be going up to his house to see him," Paddock said.

"That beautiful house on the hill?" Roosevelt asked.

"That's right," Paddock said, "but while it's beautiful on the outside the inside is, well, odd."

"In what way?" Clint asked.

"Well, it's sort of decorated like a . . . a whorehouse. I just want to warn you so you don't . . . react in a way that might insult him."

"We'll be very careful," Roosevelt said.

"Also, he's got . . . women in his house."

"A wife?" Roosevelt asked.

Paddock laughed.

"No, not a wife, just women who stay there with him."

"Is that a problem?"

"No, not as long as you know that . . . well, they

sometimes . . . well, always . . . well, they sort of . . . walk around naked.''

"Is that a fact?" Roosevelt asked. He seemed delighted with this. "Clint, will you be offended by this?"

"I think I can handle it, Teddy."

Roosevelt looked at Paddock.

"Are there any other . . . idiosyncrasies we should be concerned about?"

"I guess not . . . oh, except for one thing."

"What's that?"

"I told the Marquis you were from New York City," Paddock said. "He was real impressed with the fact that you came from somewhere civilized."

"Well," Roosevelt said, "civilized is a matter of some opinion."

"Yes, well, he expressed an interest in whether or not you played chess."

"As a matter of fact, I do."

"He's been looking for someone to play against ever since he arrived," Paddock said.

"Clint, do you play?" Roosevelt asked.

"Some," Clint said.

"May I ask a question?" Roosevelt said to Paddock.

"Go ahead."

"The Marquis wouldn't happen to have a pool table, would he?"

"No," Paddock said, "I'm afraid he hasn't."

Roosevelt looked down at the floor and said, "A pity."

As soon as Paddock left the house, the Marquis had gone in search of Denise and found her in the kitchen, chewing on cold chicken.

"There you are, my sweet," he said. "I have need of you upstairs."

"Of course," she said, and made as if to put the chicken away.

"No, no," he said, "bring it. It will add . . . flavor."

They went up to the Marquis' bedroom, which continued the bordello motif of the house. He had a huge four-poster bed with a hand-carved headboard that featured naked nymphs cavorting together. The same carvings were present on the footboard, as well.

Denise continued to eat her chicken leg while watching the Marquis undress. There was no denying that he was a handsome man in fine physical shape, and in truth he had perhaps the prettiest penis she had ever seen— especially at moments like this, when he was erect. It was his prowess in bed—and his money—that kept her there, and kept her giving in to his will. She found the decadence fun, and much better than working in a regular brothel, and she knew that the other women in the house felt the same way.

When he was naked she approached him and got on her knees in front of him. Playfully, she ran the chicken leg along his penis, covering it with the grease, and then leaned forward and proceeded to lick it off. When she had cleaned it she took his penis in her mouth and began to suck it. He groaned and reached for her head, then took the chicken leg from her and began to eat it while she continued to suck him. He had a mouthful of chicken when he finally exploded into her mouth and was careful not to spit any of it out. He was too much of a gentleman for that.

"Thank you, my love," he said as Denise got to her feet. "Please tell Angelique that we will be having guests for lunch, and tell her I will expect her to outdo herself—as always.''

''Yes, Marquis.''

''And don't forget this.''

She pouted as she accepted the chicken leg remnants and said, ''You ate it all.''

He smiled, patted her cheek, and said, ''You can get another. Off you go.''

She curtsied and withdrew from the room.

The Marquis decided he needed a bath, and then he would be ready to entertain his guests.

What, he wondered, did one wear to entertain a legend of the old West?

FORTY-NINE

It was almost a full hour later when Paddock rode up to the Marquis' house with Clint and Teddy Roosevelt. A man outside took their horses and received a warning from Clint regarding Duke, about touching him or trying to unsaddle him.

"I meant to comment before," Roosevelt said, "but that is the biggest horse I have ever seen."

"Yeah," Clint said, "he's got some size to him."

"Gentlemen," Paddock said from the steps, "this way, please."

They followed Paddock up the stairs. The front door was unlocked, and they trailed him into the house. Inside, they immediately saw what Paddock had meant about the furnishings. It truly felt as if they had just entered a San Francisco brothel.

"Impressive," Roosevelt said, and Clint didn't know

if he meant the furnishings, or the house itself.

"I think we should go this way, to the office," Paddock said, turning toward a hallway.

Just as Clint sniffed the air a man came from another room in the opposite direction and said, "Nonsense. You must come into the dining room. Lunch is served."

All three men turned to face the Marquis. He approached with his hand outstretched. Clint was surprised at his youth, and then realized that he was probably Roosevelt's age. He was wearing an expensive black suit and a white shirt with ruffles down the front and extending from the sleeves of his jacket.

"And which of you is Mr. Roosevelt?" he asked.

"That would be me," Teddy said, shaking hands.

"How nice it is to see someone from a civilized part of the world—although, in truth, I came here because I was rather weary of civilization."

"I can sympathize with you there, Marquis."

"No, no, my friend," the Marquis said, "if we are to be friends you will have to call me Antoine."

"I am Teddy."

"Teddy," the Marquis said, "what a delightful name." He released Teddy's hand and looked at Clint. "And you must be the famed Gunsmith I have heard so much about since coming to this country."

"Clint Adams is my name," Clint said, accepting the Marquis' warm handshake.

"Please, gentlemen," the Frenchman said, "come and share my table."

"Thank you," Roosevelt said. "We had not expected such a welcome."

The Marquis put his arm around Teddy's shoulders and walked him into the dining room.

"I could not be less than hospitable, eh?" he said. "Paddock, you will join us, yes?"

"I wouldn't miss it," Paddock said.

Clint looked around as they entered the dining room but didn't see any naked women. He had to admit, he was disappointed.

FIFTY

Lunch was an amazing feast. Chicken was prepared in a glaze Clint had not tasted the likes of since he was in London, his one and only trip to Europe. He had to admit—thinking back on the subject of naked women— that he wondered if the chef in the kitchen was a woman who was cooking in the nude.

He shook his head to dispel the thought and came back to the conversation the Marquis was having with Teddy Roosevelt.

There had been no talk yet of ranches or cattle or slaughterhouses or fences. The conversation had been of a more general kind, with the two more educated men talking about things Paddock and Clint found boring.

"And now, the dessert," the Marquis announced suddenly. "Angelique is the cook today. She has prepared a sumptuous dessert I think you will all enjoy. And do you like coffee?''

''Very much,'' Clint said.

''Strong?''

''The stronger the better,'' Clint said, ''and black.''

''Ah,'' the Marquis said, ''a man after my own heart.''

At that moment a woman entered carrying a tray. Clint noticed immediately that she was not naked. She was, however, beautiful. The chocolate cake she was carrying was also beautiful, and when she cut into it and placed it on plates for them, he could see that there was chocolate filling mixed with fruit—probably cherries, from the smell of it.

Next came the coffee, and just from the odor Clint could tell that it would be good.

''All right, gentlemen,'' the Marquis said, ''what is it they say in this country? Dig in?''

They did, and it was the best cake Clint had ever eaten—and also the richest. The coffee, if not the best he'd ever had, was very close.

When they were finished with dessert the Marquis said, ''Perhaps we should go into the study for some brandy, and you gentlemen can tell me why it was you wanted to meet me, eh?''

He stood, and they all followed as he left the dining room and walked across the entry foyer to a set of double sliding doors. He opened the doors, and they entered the study, which was furnished more like the Marquis' office than his bedroom or the plush living room.

''You will all have brandy?''

They all agreed, and the Marquis poured and handed each of them a glass.

"Now," he said, "please, explain what it is I can do for you."

"Well, sir," Roosevelt said, "I have recently become a partner in—"

Roosevelt stopped short as a woman entered the room. She was tall and blond, with her hair cut very short like a man's. Her face was lovely, though not beautiful. Her features were too sharp for that, but taken separately a man would find nothing to complain about.

The same could be said for her body. She was full-bodied, with round, firm breasts and buttocks that were on full display, for finally here was one of the naked women Paddock had spoken of.

Clint looked at Roosevelt, who seemed stunned by the woman's entrance. Paddock seemed amused by Roosevelt's reaction.

"Ah, Adrienne," the Marquis said. "I am doing business, my love. What is it?"

"I'm sorry," the woman said, smiling at all the men. "I didn't mean to interrupt."

"Come here, *cheri*," the Marquis said, opening one arm so she could walk into his embrace. He closed the arm around her and settled his hand on her naked breast.

"Gentlemen, this enchanting creature is Adrienne," he said. "Say hello to my new friends, Adrienne."

"It's a pleasure to meet you all," she said.

"Of course, you know Mr. Paddock."

"Yes."

It was clear to Clint from the way she said that one word that, although she knew Mr. Paddock, she certainly did not like him.

"Now, what is it, my love?"

"We were wondering," she said, "Denise and I, if

you would be needing us to, uh, entertain your guests.''

''Gentlemen?'' the Marquis asked. ''Are we in need of entertainment?''

''Uh,'' Roosevelt said, ''I don't, uh, think so—are we in need of entertainment, Clint?''

''I don't think so, Teddy,'' Clint said. ''Not today.''

''No, uh,'' Roosevelt said, turning to the Marquis, ''not today . . . uh, thank you.''

''There you go, my love,'' the Marquis said. ''You and Denise may do what you wish.''

''Thank you, Marquis.''

He slapped her rump as she walked away, and all of the men in the room watched the way her flesh quivered.

''Lovely girl,'' the Marquis said.

''Yes,'' Roosevelt said, ''she is.''

''You may have her, if you like.''

''What?''

''I share what is mine with my friends,'' the Frenchman said. ''She is yours. You only have to say the word.''

''I don't think my wife would approve, to tell you the truth,'' Roosevelt said.

''Mr. Adams?'' the Marquis asked.

''I don't think so,'' Clint said. ''I prefer to find my own women, thanks.''

''Then we should get back to business, shouldn't we?'' the Marquis asked.

''Yes,'' Roosevelt said. ''As I said, I am a partner in the Maltese Cross Ranch, and I have been told that your intention is to own most of the land around us.''

''Oh, you have been misinformed,'' the Frenchman said.

"Really?" Roosevelt asked. "In what way?"

"I do not only intend to own the land around you," the Marquis de Mores said, "I fully intend to own your land, as well."

FIFTY-ONE

Clint saw a look come over Roosevelt's face that he hadn't seen before.

"I didn't buy into a ranch just to have you take it away," he said to the Marquis.

"I will offer a fair price."

"I'm not interested in selling."

"Perhaps your partners will feel differently."

"I doubt it."

"It does not matter," the Marquis said. "Eventually you will sell."

"I don't think so."

"Everyone does, *mon ami*," the Frenchman said. "It's just a matter of the right price."

"I've got all the money I need, my friend," Roosevelt said. "What I want now is a ranch, and I've got one."

The Marquis frowned.

"I am sorry to hear this," he said seriously. "It distresses me to think that you and I will be on opposing sides. I had hoped we would be friends."

"I don't think I can be friends with somebody who is trying to take what is mine," Roosevelt said.

"And I understand this perfectly," the Frenchman said. "And you, Mr. Adams?"

"What about me?"

"You are not a partner?"

"No."

"What is your interest, then?"

"I'm friends with the owners."

"And you would be willing to help them keep their ranch?" the man asked.

"In any way I can."

"What if I offered you money?" the Marquis asked. "A lot of money to come and work for me, eh? What would your reply be?"

"No."

"Ah, are you like your friend, Mr. Roosevelt, then?" the Frenchman asked. "Do you, too, have all the money you need?"

"No, I don't," Clint said, "but I don't need yours."

"Clint has access to as much of my money as he'd ever need," Roosevelt said, which was news to Clint.

"Gentlemen," the Marquis said, "I believe we have reached the point in our conversation where we have no more to say to one another."

"I think I agree," Roosevelt said.

"I do not wish to be rude, but Mr. Paddock will show you out, eh?"

Both Clint and Roosevelt looked at Paddock.

"This way, gents."

"Thanks for lunch," Roosevelt said, and he and Clint followed Paddock to the front door.

Paddock walked all the way out with them and waited until they had their horses.

"Take some advice," he said.

"What advice?" Roosevelt asked.

"Don't try to buck him," Paddock said. "Sell out."

"I can't do that," Roosevelt said.

"Maybe your partners will," Paddock said. "If they decide to do it, they can sell their shares, which are bigger than yours."

"Perhaps," Roosevelt said, "but I have enough money to buy them out myself, if that's what they want. You see, Mr. Paddock, I have enough money to fight your Frenchman that way."

"There are other ways of fighting," Paddock said.

"That's where I come in," Clint said.

Paddock and Clint exchanged a long look.

"I know your reputation, Adams," Paddock said, "but even you couldn't stand against a dozen guns."

"This could get out of hand, Paddock," Clint said. "If your boss hires a dozen guns, Mr. Roosevelt could do the same. Hell, I've got that many friends who would come in and help, and for what? A small piece of land?"

"By the time he's done," Paddock said, "the Maltese Cross will be right in the center of everything he owns."

"Maybe," Roosevelt said.

"What do you mean?" Paddock asked.

"What if I buy up the land around the Maltese Cross myself?" Roosevelt asked. "What if I start expanding the boundaries of the Maltese Cross?"

''Then Adams is right,'' Paddock said. ''This could really get out of hand.''

''Talk to your . . . partner, Paddock,'' Clint said. ''See if you can't convince him there's a peaceful way to co-exist.''

''There's only one problem with that,'' E. G. Paddock said.

''What's that?'' Clint asked.

''I'm not sure I believe that, myself.''

Clint and Roosevelt watched Paddock walk back upstairs and go inside.

''Do you want to be a rancher this bad?'' Clint asked Roosevelt as they rode away.

''It's the principle of the thing, Clint.''

''Your principles might get a lot of people killed, Teddy.''

''Somehow,'' Roosevelt said, ''I don't feel that the entire blame for that would fall on my shoulders.''

FIFTY-TWO

Paddock went back inside and found the Marquis in his office.

"What did they say outside?" the Frenchman asked.

"Roosevelt said he could fight you dollar for dollar," Paddock said.

"And Mr. Adams?"

"He said he could fight you gun for gun."

The Marquis thought that over for a few moments, seating himself behind his desk.

"Then there must be a third option," he said finally.

"And what would that be?" Paddock asked.

"I do not know," the Marquis said. "I have not thought of it yet."

"You will," Paddock said.

"Of that I have no doubt," the Marquis de Mores said. "And what of you, Paddock?"

"What about me?"

"Where will you stand in all of this?"

"Where I've stood right from the beginning."

"With me?"

"No," Paddock said, turning to leave, "with me."

As Paddock left the Marquis knew that the man would back him all the way. After all, he had the power, and the money, and above all, Paddock worshiped money.

Now all he had to do was come up with that third option.

FIFTY-THREE

"He's crazy," Sylvane Ferris said.

"I knew it," Merrifield said. "I knew he was gonna come after us eventually. Now you've pushed it."

He was accusing Roosevelt.

"If he was going to do it eventually," Clint asked, "what's the difference?"

"He's crazy," Sylvane said again. "He thinks he can own this whole valley."

"I've got the money to fight him," Roosevelt said, "if you are both willing."

"What good is money," Merrifield asked, "against guns?"

"I've got the money to buy as many guns as he can," Roosevelt said.

"I don't know," Merrifield said.

"What don't you know?" Sylvane asked.

"I don't know if I want to die for a little piece of land."

"It's more than a little piece," Sylvane said, "it's our piece. I'm not giving up the Maltese Cross without a fight."

"Then you won't sell to him?" Roosevelt asked.

"I won't," Sylvane said, and then looked at his partner.

"Well," Merrifield said, "if you won't, I won't." Then he looked at Clint. "Will you help us?"

"As much as I can," Clint said. "I've run into too many men like this Marquis, who think that all it takes is money to get what they want."

"Don't blame the money," Roosevelt was quick to say, "blame the man."

"Oh, I know that," Clint said, "but put the man and the money together and usually you've got one arrogant son of a bitch."

"I can't argue with that," Roosevelt said. "I'm dealing with them in New York all the time."

"This ain't New York," Sylvane said. "You better know what you're getting into here, Teddy."

"He's right, Teddy," Clint said. "This is not like the battles you've fought on the floor of the Assembly. This could get bloody."

"I know that," Roosevelt said. "I'm in it for the duration."

"Then so are we," Sylvane said.

"What about Joe?" Merrifield asked. "Will he throw in with us?"

"Joe's my brother," Sylvane said, "but I can't speak for him. He'll make up his own mind."

Roosevelt looked at Clint.

"You talked about friends of yours who would come if you called?" Roosevelt said. "We'll have to decide how much to pay—"

"Whoa, Teddy," Clint said, "you don't want to be the first one to start importing guns. That tends to make you look wrong."

"So we have to wait for him to bring in gunmen?" Roosevelt asked.

"That's about the size of it," Clint said, "but I tell you what I will do. I'll send some telegrams and have some men be on alert. The moment we call them and say we need them, they'll be on the way."

"Who will you approach?" Roosevelt asked excitedly. "Bat Masterson?"

"I'm sure Bat will be one of them, yes," Clint said. "I'll have to think about it for a while, though."

"We better go into town and get some supplies," Sylvane said.

"Somebody will have to be here at all times," Clint said. "Since I'm going into town to send some telegrams, I might as well shop, too. The rest of you can stay here. Just let me know what kind of ammunition you all need."

"Shouldn't one of us go with you?" Roosevelt asked.

"No," Clint said. "You'd be a walking target in town."

"And so will you."

"Yeah," Clint said, "but I'm used to it."

FIFTY-FOUR

Armed with everyone's shopping list, Clint rode Duke into town. He stopped first at the telegraph office and sent off ten telegrams. He'd used the time riding into town to make a mental list of the men he'd need for something like this. Most of them were friends, some of them were simply men who owed him something.

Clint was aware that he could have walked out of this confrontation very easily. As he had said many times already, he was not a partner in this venture. He had no real stake except for his friendship with Merrifield, and with Roosevelt. In fact, when he analyzed it, Merrifield was more of an acquaintance than a friend. It was Roosevelt he felt an obligation to, as a friend. Also, he felt that he and Sylvane had become friends. He couldn't very well ride out and leave them to face the Marquis and whatever force he managed to put together. That was just something that was not an option for him.

When he finished sending his telegrams he walked Duke over to the general store, hoping that he wouldn't find either of the Varney brothers there. The last thing he needed right now was a confrontation with them.

As he entered he saw Marie Varney struggling with a heavy box, and he rushed to help her before she dropped it, or hurt herself.

She was surprised when he took the weight from her, and she whirled around to see who her helper was.

"You!"

"Where do you want this?" he asked.

"Over there."

He put the box where she wanted it and turned to face her. She used her wrist to brush hair from her face, and he could see that she was sweating. Her face was gleaming, and her dress was damp in patches, making it cling to her body. Also, he could smell her sweat, and it worked on him better than the finest perfume could have.

He was ready.

And so was she.

"Come in the back," she said huskily.

"What if—"

"They won't be back for a while," she said. "Come in the back, damn it."

Her insistence worked as an extra aphrodisiac, and he followed her into the small storeroom.

Once in the back she whirled and came into his arms. They kissed and he felt her heart pounding, as was his own. Suddenly, and without warning, this woman had him more excited than he had been in some time.

He bent her backward so he could kiss her neck, and her breasts through her dress. Her nipples were so hard that he was able to bite them through the fabric of her dress.

Suddenly she pushed away from him and backed off. Her breath was coming faster and faster, but she put out a hand to hold him off.

"I'm sweaty," she said. "I . . . stink . . ."

"No, you don't," he said. "Come here, Marie."

She surprised him then. Both hands went to her dress and she pulled it open, so that the buttons went flying. He knew then how he'd been able to fasten his teeth to her nipples beneath her dress. She wore no underclothes.

"Too hot . . ." she said, reading his mind.

He closed the distance between them and took her in his arms again. While kissing her, he helped her peel off her dress. She helped him with his clothes, and then they were both naked. He laid his gun belt aside, aware that her husband or his brother could walk in at any time, but that didn't seem to matter.

Her flesh was damp, but smooth and lovely. Her nipples were dark brown and distended. His kisses brought her gooseflesh, chilling her even as she sweated some more.

He pushed her down on a small stack of boxes, spread her legs wide, and entered her in one swift movement. She caught her breath and cried out. If there were any customers out front, they were going to wonder what was going on.

He began to move in and out of her while standing, his hands on her knees, holding her wide apart.

"Oh, God . . ." she gasped. "I knew this was going to happen the first time I saw you."

He realized that he knew it, too. That was probably

why he'd gotten so angry with Sylvane for suggesting it.

"Ooh, yes, Jesus . . ." she moaned, her nails scratching at the boxes beneath her. Then she said, "Wait, wait . . ." and pushed him away.

"Wha—" he started, but she surprised him again by turning over on her belly and lifting her ass to him.

"This way," she said. "Hurry."

He wasn't quite sure what she wanted, but she reached for him, grasped him, pulled him between her thighs and up into her again. He started to move again, his hands on her glorious ass. Her breath was coming hard now, rasping in her throat. It had become oppressively hot in that storeroom, and her perspiration was flowing, along with his.

He was slamming into her so hard now that he was grunting, and she was moaning and trying not to cry out. At last he felt her body shudder, and she literally bit into her hand to keep from screaming. Moments later he exploded into her and had to bite his lip to keep from bellowing. . . .

She pulled her dress back on, then realized the buttons were gone.

"I'll have to change," she said.

"Marie—"

She put her hand out to stop him.

"Don't say anything," she said. "I don't care if it never happens again. I'm just glad it happened this time."

He started to dress, but his flesh was too damp.

"There's a trough out back," she said. "I'm going to

change. I'll meet you back in the store and we can finish whatever business you came to conduct.''

"Marie—"

''I don't want to talk now!'' she snapped. ''I need to change before they come back.''

He nodded and went out the back door with his boots and trousers on, but not his shirt. He went to the trough and washed his torso in it. He had nothing to dry himself with, but the sun would dry him in a few moments. He put his gun belt back on and looked around. It was probably a miracle that the Varneys hadn't come back and found them rutting in the back room, or that someone else hadn't come in.

Maybe Marie Varney didn't care if it ever happened again, but Clint wanted the woman again, even now, moments after he'd had her. He wanted her in a bed, though, in a place where they both wouldn't be sweating like animals. He didn't often have sex with another man's wife, but with Marie Varney that didn't seem to matter.

He was dry enough now that he could put his shirt back on. Fully dressed he walked around the building so he could once again enter through the front door, as if nothing had happened.

FIFTY-FIVE

He walked into the store and saw Marie standing behind the counter. She was wearing a dress that looked just like the one she had on before, only this one still had the buttons.

There was someone else in the store, though.

"Mr. Adams," she said as he entered, "what can I do for you?"

Off to the side Zack Varney, her husband, turned and looked at him. Jesus, Clint thought, when did he come in? Was he staring at Clint like he knew something?

"Whataya want?" Varney demanded finally.

"I've got a list," Clint said.

"You got cash?"

"I've got money."

Varney stared hard at Clint, then looked at his wife.

"Give the list to her," Varney said. "Fill it, Marie. I'm goin' to the saloon."

He headed for the door, then stopped short and turned around.

"Make sure he pays," he said to his wife. "No credit for him or anybody from the Maltese Cross."

"Sure, Zack."

Varney turned and left.

"I'm sorry . . ." she said.

"When did he get here?"

"A minute or so ago, that's all. He wasn't here when I came back in."

"Good."

"Why?" she asked, taking the list from him. She talked while she walked around and filled the list. "You're not afraid of him, I know that."

"No, I'm not."

"So why would you care if he walked in on us?"

"Would you care?"

"No."

"Why not?"

She set the boxes of shells on the counter in front of Clint, enough for everyone's weapons at the Maltese Cross.

"Because maybe then he'd let me go," she said. "Or maybe you would have killed him."

"Is that what you want, Marie?" he asked. "Somebody to kill your husband?"

"It wouldn't hurt."

"Well, don't look to me for that," Clint said. "I don't usually have sex with married women, and I'm sure as hell not going to kill anyone's husband."

"I know that," she said. "Don't you think I know that?"

"I don't know what you want, or what you know, Marie," he said. "Do you?"

"No," she said, "I don't, except that I want you to pay for these supplies."

"How much?"

She told him and he paid her.

"Tell your friends I'm sorry, but I can't extend them any more credit."

"I'll tell them."

He didn't tell her that with Roosevelt as their partner they weren't going to need any more credit.

"Marie . . . why don't you just leave?"

She leaned on the counter.

"And go where?"

"Anywhere."

"That takes money," she said. "Are you gonna give me some money?"

"No."

"Well, neither is anyone else," she said, "so I guess I'm just stuck here."

He left, with neither of them referring again to what had happened in the back room.

However, they were both wondering if it was ever going to happen again.

FIFTY-SIX

Later that day Clint discovered one of the conditions of Roosevelt's investment in the Maltese Cross Ranch.

"We have to go to Minnesota," Sylvane told him, "and break our contract with our man there."

"Why?"

"Teddy doesn't want us to have any other partners."

"And you're willing to go along with that?"

"Of course," Sylvane said. "He has enough money for us to do what we want to do."

"And Merrifield agreed to this, as well?"

"Yes."

"When are you leaving?"

"Tomorrow," Sylvane said. "We will telegraph Teddy when the deal is done, and then return."

They were sitting in the Maltese Cross house, Sylvane

257

and Clint, both having coffee. Roosevelt was out riding the ranch with Merrifield.

"This is what Roosevelt wants," Sylvane said. "He's even going to buy the stock we already have from the Minnesota people."

"It's up to him what he wants to do with his money," Clint said, "but if the Marquis decides to make a move while you're gone, we'll be two men short."

"Do you want us to stay, then?"

Clint rubbed his chin as he thought.

"I can't predict what that Frenchman is going to do," Clint said, "unless . . ."

"Unless what?"

"Unless he's guided by Paddock," Clint said. "He is more the kind of man I *could* predict."

"And what do you think Paddock would do?"

"I think the joker in their deck is me," Clint said. "If I wasn't around they would probably handle things very differently."

"So you think Paddock will suggest trying to get rid of you?"

Clint nodded.

"How?"

"Well," Clint said, "they already tried buying me off. That leaves one thing."

"Killing you?"

"Yes."

"You think Paddock will try it himself?"

"Not alone."

"Then I think we should stay," Sylvane said.

"No," Clint said, "I think you should go."

"But you just said—"

"I'm thinking without you around, maybe Paddock will make a try for me."

Sylvane nodded and said, "I see, and you'll be waiting for him."

"And once we can prove that he tried to kill me, you can use that information to keep the Marquis off your backs."

"Because everybody knows Paddock works for the Marquis."

Clint nodded.

"We can either go to the sheriff in Mandan, or the U.S. marshal."

"The marshal, I think," Sylvane said. "The sheriff was already involved in the O'Donald, Luffsey, and Wannegan business."

"The marshal it is, then."

"Will you send him a telegram?"

"No," Clint said, "you will. If I send it from here, the Frenchman will know about it. You and Merrifield send it somewhere down the line on your way to Minnesota."

"What if Paddock doesn't try for you, and the marshal shows up?" Sylvane asked. "What will you tell him?"

"I guess I'll figure that out when the time comes," Clint said.

That evening E. G. Paddock and the Marquis were in the Frenchman's office, discussing the subject of the Maltese Cross Ranch.

"I was not going to concern myself with them for some time yet," the Marquis said, "but it seems the time has come."

"What do you want to do?" Paddock asked.

"This is your country," the Frenchman said. "How would you suggest we deal with it?"

"Well, first off I think we got to get rid of Adams," Paddock said. "He's too dangerous."

"I can send for some men—"

"No," Paddock said, "if we try to send a telegram he might hear about it."

"Is there someone in town you can use to help you with him?"

"I think there is," Paddock said. "Adams had a run-in with the Varney brothers, I heard."

"Who are they?"

"They own the general store."

"Ah," the Marquis said, "one of them is married to the stunning woman who works in the store?"

"That's right."

"And will they cooperate with you?"

"I'm sure they will," Paddock said, "with the right motivation."

"Do it, then," the Marquis said, "and do it soon."

"I'll go into town and talk to them tonight," Paddock said. "We might be able to solve our problem by tomorrow."

"Good," the Frenchman said, "I like quick solutions. If you get this done for me, there will also be quick rewards—and I do not only mean money."

Paddock knew that he was referring to one of the women in the house, which suited him just fine. He'd been waiting a long time for another opportunity with that little Denise.

He stood up and said, "I'll go and take care of it right now."

FIFTY-SEVEN

Paddock found willing allies in the Varney brothers. Neither one had any liking for Clint Adams, but they were afraid to move against him because of his reputation. With Paddock, however, they felt more confident.

"There'll be the three of us," Paddock said, "and two of the Marquis' aides."

"Five men against one," Zack Varney said, cackling. "Those are my kind of odds."

"When do we do this?" Len Varney asked.

"I'll let you know," Paddock said. "You'll have to be ready to go whenever I give the word."

"We'll be ready," Zack said.

"What about the others?" Len asked. "Ferris, Merrifield, and that dandy from New York."

"We'll wait until we can get Adams alone," Paddock

said. ''With his reputation nobody will be surprised when he's shot down.''

The three men shook hands, and then Paddock left the house the Varney brothers shared with Zack's wife, Marie.

Marie Varney had listened to the entire conversation from the bedroom, and now—even as her husband and his brother were shaking hands on the deal—she slipped out the window. As Paddock mounted his horse in front of the house and rode off, she went to the lean-to in back of the house, which the Varneys used as a barn, saddled her horse, and headed for the Maltese Cross Ranch to warn Clint Adams.

When the knock came at the door, Clint, Roosevelt, Sylvane, and Merrifield all stopped talking and looked at the door.

''Who could that be?'' Merrifield asked.

''I'll see,'' Clint said, and walked to the door. ''Who is it?''

''It's Marie,'' a woman's voice said, ''Marie Varney.''

''Zack Varney's wife?'' Sylvane asked, surprised.

''What does she want?'' Merrifield asked.

Clint opened the door and stepped outside, closing it behind him.

''We have to talk,'' Marie said. She was wearing one of her simple dresses. Her horse was in front of the house.

''Come inside,'' he said.

''No,'' she said, ''let's go to the barn.''

"All right," he said. "Walk your horse over and I'll be right with you."

As she did so he opened the door and stuck his head inside the house.

"I'll be back in a little while."

"What does she want?" Roosevelt asked.

"I'm going to find out."

As Clint closed the door, Sylvane chuckled and said, "I'll bet I know what she wants."

"But . . . she's another man's wife," Roosevelt said.

Merrifield and Sylvane both stared at him, and Merrifield asked, "What's your point?"

As Clint entered the barn he stopped and lit the lamp hanging on the wall next to the door. Marie was standing by a pile of hay, and in the flickering light of the lamp she was beautiful. He knew that in the right kind of dresses and gowns, she would be stunning.

"What's this all about, Marie?"

"I've got some information for you," she said breathlessly.

"What is it?"

"Before I give it to you," she said, "you have to give me something."

"What?"

In one swift movement her dress was down around her ankles, and she was naked in the yellow lamplight.

"Marie—"

Now he knew she wasn't breathless from her ride out from town.

"Come on, Clint," she said, "I know you want me. . . ."

"Of course I do, but—"

"The information I have for you is real important," she said, "but I'll only trade it."

Oh, well, he thought, approaching her, if she really wanted to trade . . .

FIFTY-EIGHT

Naked, they fell into the hay together. This time there was no perspiration. She smelled sweet, as if she'd taken a bath after work today, and as he kissed her breasts and nipples and kissed his way down her body he could smell her readiness. When his head was between her legs and his mouth and tongue were working on her, getting her wetter and wetter, she moaned and bucked beneath him.

"Oh, God, you're killing me," she said, holding his head in place. "Jesus, nobody's ever done this . . . to me . . . stop, stop, I'm . . . I'm gonna . . . die . . . ohhh . . ."

He stopped, but not because he thought she'd die. He mounted her and slid into her so easily because she was so slick and hot. She wrapped her long legs around his back and reached for him with her arms, pulling him to her as tightly as possible.

"Oh, yes, please . . . don't stop . . ." she moaned as he moved in and out of her. He reached between them and touched her while he was still inside of her, and she let out such a shriek that he wondered if they heard it at the house.

Around them the horses were beginning to become agitated. Clint found himself thinking that he was glad Joe Ferris's pinto wasn't present.

She was so slick and wet and becoming wetter still that her scent filled the barn. Clint wondered if the horses were reacting to her feminine smell. Duke was calm, but he was a gelding.

Clint quickened his pace and she moved with him, her butt banging up and down on the bed of hay. Suddenly, she clung to him, nails digging into him, and he knew she was nearing her time. He began to take her in long, hard strokes, for his benefit, not hers, and as she shuddered and bit into his shoulder to keep from screaming he exploded inside of her and bit back a shout of his own. . . .

"What's the information you have, Marie?" he asked moments later.

"No, wait . . ." she said, reaching for him as he stood up to get dressed.

"There are three men in that house who are going to come looking for me, Marie," he said, reaching for his trousers. "You better get dressed, too."

"I can't," she said.

"Why not?"

"I can't feel my legs," she said, lying back on the

hay with her hands behind her head. This thrust her breasts toward him, the nipples still hard, and he turned away so she couldn't see that he was reacting to her again.

"Clint, no man's ever done this to me before," she said. "I mean, these feelings, I never have them with Zack, or Len—"

"Len?" he asked, looking at her. "You've had sex with your husband's brother?"

"Well, of course," she said, her tone mocking, "they share everything . . ."

"He gives you to his brother?" he demanded.

Suddenly she looked away, ashamed.

"Marie—"

"They're going to come for you," she said, cutting him off. She sat up and reached for her dress. It was out of her reach, though, so Clint picked it up and tossed it to her.

"Who's coming for me?"

"Len and Zack and some other men."

"What other men?"

"I don't know," she said, "I just know what Mr. Paddock told them tonight."

"Paddock was with them tonight?"

"Yes," she said. "He said he needed help killing you. He said they'd be five against one, and they'd wait until you were alone."

"You came to warn me about that?"

"Yes."

"What will happen when they find that you're gone?" he asked.

"I don't know," she said with a shrug. "I'll probably get a beating when I go back . . ."

"Don't go back, Marie."

"What? Where am I supposed to go?"

"Get on your horse and ride, and keep riding until you reach a town."

"I can't just ride without knowing where I'm going," she said. "Besides, I have no money."

Clint, dressed by now, took all the money he had from his pocket and gave it to her.

"But—"

"There's a town called Mandan, one hundred and fifty miles east of here. Go there, get a hotel room, and wait for me. From there I'll help you get to San Francisco."

"San Francisco?"

"That's where a woman as beautiful as you are belongs, Marie."

She stood up, straightened her dress, and buttoned it.

"Just like that?"

"You want to leave, don't you?"

"Yes, but they won't just let me—"

"Marie," he said, "if they come after me with guns, they'll probably be dead before they know it."

"Then why do I have to leave?" she asked. "Can't I stay here with you?"

"No," he said, "there're three other men here. Ride for Mandan. If you come to a town before then, stop and wait there for me."

"How long?" she asked. "How long do I wait?"

"Until I come."

"What if you don't?"

"I will," he said, "I promise."

She looked away.

"Men have made promises to me before."

"I'll keep mine."

She looked at the money in her hand.

"If you stay in a hotel, and take your meals there, you have enough money for a week. When I get there I'll buy you clothes and put you on a train to San Francisco."

"Y-you won't be coming with me?"

"No," he said, "I can't, but I have friends who will meet you at the other end and help you get settled. I swear, Marie, I'll help you."

"I can't ride tonight—"

"You'll stay with me tonight here in the barn," he said, "and in the morning you can be on your way."

That seemed to clinch it for her.

"All right," she said, "a-all right, I'll do it."

"Good," he said. "Unsaddle your horse and take care of him, and get comfortable. I'll be back in a little while. I have to talk to the others."

"Clint?"

"Yes?"

"Thank you."

"Thank you," he said, touching her shoulder. "You're the one who came here to help me, and I appreciate it."

He left the barn to tell the others about her warning.

FIFTY-NINE

In the morning Clint put Bill Merrifield, Sylvane Ferris, and Teddy Roosevelt on the train. Prior to that he had sent Marie Varney on her way on horseback.

Once the train had pulled out he headed back to the Maltese Cross Ranch.

A man who worked at the train station knocked on E. G. Paddock's door minutes later.

"Yes?"

"They got on a train."

"Who?"

"All of 'em," the man said. "Ferris, Merrifield, and that New York dandy."

"Not Adams?"

The man shook his head.

"He stayed behind."

271

"Where were they going?"

"Minnesota."

Paddock paid the man, then saddled his horse and rode to the Marquis' house.

"He's alone," Paddock told the Marquis, "at the ranch."

"Where did the others go?"

"Their final destination is Minnesota."

"So then you'll do it tonight."

"Yes," Paddock said. "I have the Varney brothers, but I'll need the same two men we used in June against O'Donald and the others."

"You'll have them."

"Do you want to be in on this?"

"No," the Frenchman said, "not this time. You handle it."

Paddock nodded and left, thinking about little Denise's naked breasts.

That night Clint sat by the front window and waited. He knew they'd come tonight. He had his rifle across his legs, and his modified Colt on his hip. The opportunity to catch him alone would be too good to pass up. If he knew Paddock—and he knew men *like* Paddock— they would be coming tonight.

Paddock, the Varney brothers, and two of the Marquis' aides whose names Paddock didn't even know crept closer to the house under the cover of darkness.

"Len, you and your brother take the front," Paddock said. Then he turned to the other men and said, "You two take the back."

"And you?" Len Varney asked.

"Don't worry," Paddock said. "I'll be here."

"And we're gettin' paid for this, right?" Zack Varney asked.

"Yes," Paddock said, "you're getting paid."

Len nudged his brother and said, "Let's go."

"Don't anybody shoot," Paddock said, "until I fire. Got it?"

They all understood.

"Then let's go," he said.

Paddock had almost decided to simply ambush Clint Adams whenever they could, but this way was just as good. His horse was in the barn, and he was trapped in the house. There was no way he could get away.

Clint heard Duke and knew that someone had either entered the barn, or took a look inside. It was all the warning he needed.

Paddock gave the men time to move into place, then squatted behind the broken-down corral and called out, "Adams? You in there?"

"I'm here, Paddock."

"Got something for you out here," Paddock said. "Why don't you come out and get it?"

"Okay," Clint said, "I'm coming out," and he threw the door open.

This totally surprised and confused Paddock. He didn't think Clint would actually come out. This took the Marquis' two aides out of the play for now, because they were behind the house. Paddock had planned on two men breaking into the house in the back, and two in the front.

"Get him!" he shouted. "Get him!"

Zack Varney looked at his brother and said, "But he ain't fired yet."

"There's Adams," Len said. "Get him."

The hesitation of the Varney brothers worked in Clint's favor. He stepped out and threw himself to the ground before any shots were fired.

Paddock, seeing this, realized that his instructions to the others had been not to fire until he did. Hastily, he pulled his guns and fired them both at Clint.

The Varneys began to fire, as well.

Behind the house the two men heard the shots and started running at the house. Men stepped out from behind the trees on either side of them—Sylvane from the right and Roosevelt from the left—and Roosevelt shouted, "Stop right there."

Confused, the two men turned and pointed their guns, but Sylvane and Roosevelt fired first. The two men were dead before they could get off a shot.

Paddock heard the shooting from behind the house and knew things had gone wrong, somehow. When he saw Bill Merrifield and Joe Ferris step from the trees he holstered his guns, turned, and ran for his horse, leaving the Varneys to face Clint, Ferris, and Merrifield.

As the Varneys fired, Clint picked up the flash from their guns and returned the fire. Bill Merrifield and Sylvane's brother Joe came out from behind the trees to his left and also began to fire.

"Shit!" Len Varney said. "He's got help."

"Where's Paddock?" Zack asked. "Where are the others?"

"We're on our own," Len said.

"Let's get out of here."

They stood to flee, tossing shots Clint's way to cover themselves, but all they did was make themselves easy targets. A bullet from Clint's gun plowed into Zack's chest, stopping his heart immediately, and a slug from Merrifield's gun took Len in the throat, dropping him to the ground where he lay, making horrible gurgling sounds.

Clint and Merrifield ran to the fallen men. Joe Ferris ran around back to check on his brother.

"Zack's dead," Clint said, leaning over the body.

Merrifield looked at him, then down at Len.

"This one's alive, but not for long. He's drowning in his own blood."

Clint leaned over Len and saw that Merrifield was right. Blood was pouring from Len Varney's mouth.

"Len," he said, "we may be able to get you to a doctor, but you've got to tell me who brought you here. Was it Paddock?"

Wide-eyed, the man nodded his head while holding both hands around his throat to try to stem the tide of blood from the wound. Most of the blood, however, still seemed to be coming from his mouth.

"You saw that," Clint said to Merrifield. "He identified Paddock."

"Clint," Merrifield said, "we can't get him to a doctor before he drowns."

"I know."

They both looked down at him. At that moment the two Ferris brothers and Teddy Roosevelt came around from behind the house.

"The other two are dead," Sylvane said, looking down at Len Varney.

"That's a horrible way to die," Teddy Roosevelt said.

"I know," Clint said, and shot Len Varney between the eyes.

EPILOGUE

Clint and Teddy Roosevelt watched as Duke was loaded on the stock car of the train.

"I don't think the Marquis will be bothering you too much, Teddy," Clint said. "Not for a while, anyway."

"Probably not as long as the marshal is still looking for Paddock."

"Or until he finds Paddock."

"Of course," Roosevelt said, "the Marquis might have taken care of that already. He wouldn't want Paddock identifying him, would he?"

Clint thought about the other men who had disappeared back in June—O'Donald and Wannegan—and said, "No, he wouldn't."

They walked toward the passenger car.

"I have to admit," Roosevelt said, "it was a simple but effective plan to draw Paddock out, making it look like the rest of us left town. It was an easy thing for us to stop the train and get off right outside of town."

"I knew if he thought I was completely alone he'd come for me."

"You know the Western mind, Clint," Roosevelt said, "I have to give you that."

"And what about you, Teddy?" Clint asked. They stopped in front of the passenger car. "Do you prefer the West or the East?"

"I can't tell you for sure yet," Roosevelt said, taking a deep breath. "This country is beautiful and I find the West very exciting, but I've also got plans for my political future."

"Big plans?" Clint asked.

Roosevelt smiled and said, "Perhaps someday, the biggest. For now, though, I think I'll be staying here a little longer, at least until the ranch begins to prosper. Sure you don't want to stay awhile, Clint?" Roosevelt asked. "It might be fun."

"I've had all the fun I can stand," Clint said. "Besides, I made a promise to a lady, and I intend to keep it."

"Well," Teddy said, "I'll either be here or in New York. If you get back either way, make damned sure you look me up."

They shook hands.

"You still have to give me a chance to get even at pool."

"One of these days, Teddy," Clint said, "one of these days."

Watch for

TEXAS WIND

193rd novel in the exciting GUNSMITH series
from Jove

Coming in February!